The Destined Destinies

(A Romantic story)

Sushen Biswas

The Destined Destinies

Sushen Biswas

Published by Sushen K. Biswas, 2024.

This is a work of fiction. Similarities to real people, places, or events are entirely coincidental.

THE DESTINED DESTINIES

First edition. November 17, 2024.

Copyright © 2024 Sushen Biswas.

ISBN: 979-8227498359

Written by Sushen Biswas.

This book of Destined Destinies is dedicated to my wife Susmita Mondal who owns the copyright when I am no more on the earth.

"Things that I longed for in vain

and things that I got---let them pass.

Let me but truly possess the things

that I ever spurned and overlooked."

--- Rabindranath Tagore

THE DESTINED DESTINIES
Part- One

Chapter 1

Animesh's belief paid him alright. God smiled on him once again for his efforts. It was mid-November, another pleasant day for him in two years' time. He was at the SSC office compound. It was here that he had been a few times a year before for the viva test and later for the result when it was published. Now he was here to see the SSC results of the written examinations. He passed the exam.

Colleagues in school frequently pricked at him about it. He often heard them say: "Animesh-babu is going to leave us behind and go away. Sometimes they said: You'll certainly go near your home this time."

Animesh smiled and lightly said in reply, "It's like 'counting the chickens before they are hatched. Don't you be so excited about it until it comes true!"

He wouldn't want to believe it until he found that he was really appointed to a suitable place.

After the viva, when he was empanelled and the news was out to them, they repeated the sentences with an emphatic tone: "This time we can't hold you back anymore."

Animesh smiled a dormant happiness to welcome their comments but tried to make it light saying, "Let the appointment letter come and see where I'm posted." His hope of re-starting the English teaching class again came alive.

At the end of the weekend, at an ungodly hour when the shrill squeaks of the alarm clock went for 3:30 a.m., a heavy wave of even deeper sleep got him badly and he felt like getting into a real blissful slumber instead of quitting the bed. He felt so lazy that he didn't even feel like stirring in bed. It happened every time for about two years when the alarm rang.

He brought himself up from the bed very lazily and sat up for a few minutes with his eyes closed, and consoled himself: "a few weeks more and then I wouldn't have to take all these troubles of getting out of the imperfect sleep and rush back to the box-like, airless, lightless damp room on the ground floor of New Burdwan Hotel and go to 'that school'.

He got out of the bed bleary-eyed and put the light on, then taking paste on his toothbrush, he tottered over to the tube-well nook for a wash.

With enough time in hand, he had no rush for the bus; he listened to some music on the cassette player mindful of the time on his watch. Then locking the door, taking the valise on the shoulder, grabbing the duffel bag in his hand, walking across the yard over to his mother's room, he called her and gave her the key, and went out for Burdwan. The Amway teaching at least taught him to think positive, live positive and hope positive. Positive thinking has a great favourable power in it and it was being instilled in him.

Chapter 2

Friday was the day of the week when there were two spells of recess in his school; the first break for an hour starting after the second period of class. It was for the Muslim teachers and students to go over to the nearby Mosque to offer their Namaz (Islamic prayer) and the second one after the fifth period for ten minutes. The clamour of children playing, running about, shouting to one another was usual and they all were used to it.

When he got into the staffroom eating mixed spiced puffed rice, he noticed that the Khan brothers, P.K, and P.K.K, were talking about buying land, a one-page form half filled-in was lain under their fingers on the table. He slipped into his place and sat down looking down at the form and eating the puffed rice from the small paper-bag. He could understand nothing until Prasant Khan took the form up in his hand and looked up at him saying, "Would you like to buy land?"

"Buy land? Where?" asked Animesh chewing puffed rice, "How much is the rate?"

"It'll be at cheap price, anyway," he answered, "But you can't buy it at will. It's a township project at Ullas." He continued, "First you have to go through the lottery. If you win, you'll be entitled to buy it. Do you wanna have a go? Think of it."

"I'm not interested, 'cos I can't afford, actually," Animesh said seriously. He knew he couldn't afford the money it needed.

P. K.K. was busy with his own form. He suddenly said out, "Why worry? You'll get a bank loan. I'll have a loan, too."

Animesh just made a smile. He swore truthfully. It was the Amway that ate up half of his total earnings but he received nothing in return and the rest he spent on his living with a little out of it saved.

P.K.K tried to encourage him. He reasonably explained the privileges of Burdwan town. "The new township is going to be by the junction of the by-pass G.T. Road and the old G.T road. You will get into the main town in ten minutes only, there will be schools, new offices, hospitals. Communication is excellent, and above all, it is not crowded at all. You can't have this chance again." He explained. Prasant Khan agreed with P.K.K and encouraged him too.

"Let me think it over how far I can get to," Animesh said casually.

He turned the matter over and over in his mind but he didn't get any positive signal from the bottom of his heart. He knew he couldn't afford it. And more to the point, he'd made up his mind that he'd go near his home for which he worked so hard. He looked forward to a new appointment.

Chapter 3

The appointment letter was sure to come and it did come to his home address. At the weekend just as he got into his room on a Saturday, a brown official letter came to his sight lying on the cluttered table. He thought it could be from the SSC office. He put down the valise on the bed, the duffel on the floor, and took up the envelope in his hand and read the sender's address on its left. His guess was right. It was from the SSC office but he wouldn't be impatient about it. He would open it comfortably a few minutes later. So, pushing the door to, and hurriedly changing his clothes, he opened the door again and scurried over to the tube well nook for a brief wash, kind of delight bubbled up in his mind while washing his face and feet.

Animesh sat on the edge of the bed next to the cluttered table pressed against the bedstead. Then taking the letter out of the envelope and unfolding it on the table, he carefully started reading the letter leaning over it with a slight palpitation in his heart.

When he was half way through, his eyes stopped short on a line and popped. He turned grave, his face grew hotter and worryingly thoughtful. "What's it do I see?" he asked himself. The hopes and joy that he had been carrying since the day he found himself empanelled at the SSC office compound was gone in a moment like camphor. The SSC office staff did him 'a great favour' he could never forget. Animesh was recommended for Sitarampur High School. It was located farther away than Asansol; from Burdwan it was another 80 kilometers away. It would even be harder for him to come back home at the weekend and go back there in the morning to catch school. His hand went up to his temple rubbing it with his fingers and gripping the bridge between the eyes hopelessly, his head hung over the letter. He felt as if his blood streams in his veins slowed down and turned cold first and then hotter and hotter rushing up to his head and face. His patience, precious time and hard labour on the exam preparations—all went in vain. It was only him that knew what it takes to come through a series of exams to have his name empanelled for a government job, especially in a corrupted country with a million unemployed young men and women crazily fighting for it. He wondered if he could be able to hold his patience for another SSC exam. The phrases "Damn it!" burst out of his lips instinctively, "Shit!" He shook his head. "Nothing in shit favourable will come to my lot." He called the SSC names as hard as he could casting a fierce look on the letter at that moment and then he felt like tearing it to bits and letting it go flying, or he felt like crushing it into a ball and hurling it away with all his kinetic force. But he didn't do anything of that sort. It wasn't the letter that deceived him but the government. He remained still, stiff and grave, the hard gaze was still down on the letter. He was hurt beneath badly.

It was then his mother got in with some refreshment. She held it to him. "Here you are," she said very softly that it was hardly heard, holding the bowl towards him. "Like to have tea now?" she asked. He took the bowl from his mother's hand silently and put it down beside the pile of the books on the table. He shook his head lightly, "No," he breathed out the answer. Then folding the letter lazily, he slipped it back into the envelope and threw it on the table disgustingly. The thought of his exiled posting kept on running in his head while eating the bread toast gravely, and slowly. Though he was hungry and tired, he couldn't eat it.

The weekend holiday ended. He was back to school. The staffroom of the school was not yet full with teachers and non-teaching staff when he got in. After the prayer of the national anthem on the ground, they were in the staff room when Prasant Khan first asked him about his new posting: "By the way, what's your news? Where have you been posted?"

Animesh stumbled over the answer for he didn't want to answer simply and directly.

"Which school have you been given?" he asked again.

"Which school!" Animesh expressed hopelessness. He'd already expressed his boiling anger at every place to everybody whoever raised the painful issue of his new appointment explaining to them the filthy conspiratorial deception of the SSC. His friends and well-wishers felt for him.

"A hell of a school has come to my lot," he replied grumpily pointing to his hapless forehead. "I have been exiled over to Sitarampore," he snapped.

"Sitarampore?" asked Prasant-babu, "Which school up there?"

At this moment Paran K. Khan got in wiping sweat off his face with the handkerchief listening to Animesh's irritated words.

"Belruin High School," Animesh said in reply and quickly took the letter out from inside the bag-flap and handed it to Prasant. The Khan brothers both looked down at it eagerly.

"Oh, you have got the appointment letter?" Paran-babu questioned declaratively. They scanned through it and Paran-babu shook his head and flicked his finger on the letter. "You can't go there," he said emphatically, "It's really a long way away; near the border of Bihar state. "You can't go home every time on a holiday in the middle of the week like you do from here." Prasant-babu agreed with him. Animesh listened to them silently and sadly. "I know I can't," he said agreeably. "The damned fucking shit fucked up my fortune and bungled up my hopes and peace," he burst out. "Be cool, be cool, Animesh-babu, be cool. Don't flare up like this." They said trying to soothe him. "What else can we people do when it's all up to them?" Prasant Khan commented.

"I don't want to lose my head—but think it over, the education minister and the SSC both had declared repeatedly that the teachers in service would be posted in the commuting distances. "I ate it up because I trusted those filthy deceivers. Not only did they betray me in one way but also misled me. What was the use betraying me?" he went on.

"Have a go again. It's not the end of the world," Paran-babu said in consolation.

"How come?" Animesh asked helplessly, "They'd started selling forms for the next SSC exam before they appointed the empanelled ones. How should I know they would betray me? I didn't apply to the SSC this time."

"Then there's nothing to say," Paran Khan gave up.

Prasant Khan said, "They ought to have appointed all the empanelled candidates before advertising for the next examination."

"It is a blatant deception and I will always hold them responsible for these misdoings," Animesh said excitedly and part of which was caught by Pachkori-babu, who just came in. Behind him came in other teachers—N. M, M. R. Seikh, Korrim Khan, Illias Yasmin-babu and still later came P. Dutta and Asgar Seikh Sahib.

"Who did the misdoings?" asked Pachkori-babu with a curious look around the guys.

Animesh tried to arrange the answer but before he did, Prasant-babu said, "Animesh-babu got a new appointment in a far-away school."

Then again, the same matter went on for some time with various kinds of comments and advices. All the teachers felt for him and wished 'better luck next time' but inwardly they might have thought differently that they didn't have to lose a teacher when the school still had three more vacancies at the moment. Animesh could only think that it was the Universal Super Ruler who put up the barrier for him in the way for all the ways that he took so long whenever he tried to do something—from his dream of going abroad to these SSC exams. And that many people had said that 'man makes his own good luck himself' was not felt right to him. All the same he would have more goes—"hopes springs eternal."

Chapter 4

About two months had gone by since he got the new appointment letter for Sitarampore High School and he closed the chapter by refusing to join it.

In this school the recess was going on now. After he'd had refreshments, he went over to the Headmaster's table where Illias Yasmin sir was sitting in the old wooden chair as the Teacher-in-Charge. The Headmaster had retired only a few months before. He was working away with a register book, and papers opened before him. The table was cluttered with files, registers, bunches of papers, paperweights, an ash-stray, and so on. Yasmin sir's office-work was neat and clean, and was praised by the D.I. Office of Burdwan, too. He was, in fact, a work-crazy guy. Korrim and Animesh once opined that Illias sir deserved to be a headmaster; they both wished him to be the H.M. of this school.

"Mean to say something, Animesh-babu?" he asked briefly without tearing his eyes from the register. He'd guessed well who it was.

"Yes, Sir," Animesh said looking down at the open register where his pen was running and paused briefly as if he hesitated.

"Tell me," he said in brief trying to finish the running column in the register.

"Because I failed to fulfill my expectation, I refused to join the new school in Sitarampore. So, I would like to do the B. Ed. this session, sir."

Now he looked up at him, the pen poised over the register. "Well, yeah," he said with a soft smile on his good-looking, truly gentleman's saved face that indicated kind of happiness, maybe because it was a good sign that the school was not going to lose a teacher that was received the hard way; the education department of West Bengal wouldn't post teachers at vacant posts right on demand.

"Yes, do the B. Ed. this time. And stay on in Burdwan." He began with the encouragement that he often gave him. "Burdwan is the best place in the whole district. Why think of leaving it? I'd already told you 'try buying a piece of land out there and make a humble home and be settled like Prasant-babu is doing. There are all kinds of privileges up there.'" He gave a good reasonable explanation about it and looked down back at the register where he was working. But right away he looked up at him again. "Well, you'll have to lodge in an application to the secretary through the TIC and that's all. It'll be passed before the Managing Committee and you'll be let off for B.Ed."

"All right, Sir," Animesh said pleasantly. Yasmin sir now got back to his work and Animesh to his place.

When the B-Ed-forms had been up for grabs soon, he applied for the B. Ed. Katwa was his best choice.

THE FIRST TURNING OF THE STORY
Chapter 5

Ah, yeah !" Animesh exclaimed with a deep breath out as he looked up briefly at the faded sky- blue building as he got off his bicycle at the main entrance gate. "This is the dear building where I first came about sixteen years back when the first down appeared like a light black shadow under my nose. This was where I spent my four precious years to build my career for the Higher Secondary and the B.A courses."

Yes, sixteen years back when he passed the Secondary Board Examinations. His dear school of Dainhat High School, where he had studied for six long years refused to get him admitted in the Commerce stream for the Higher Secondary courses. The Commerce stream was then the common choice and in demand for the average students while the Arts stream was considered downgraded and suitable for the ones who were good at memorizing big answers; but the school refused to let him into Commerce.

Leaving his friends there how bad he felt, how sad it made him. The school authority complained that he had poor marks in Math; indeed, he did very bad in the Math. Those days he had to do two subjects in a day for the Board Exams with one-hour break for lunch and final scan through the answers. He recalled and felt down for the good old days that had been left far behind; they would never be back once again.

Turning on to his right, walking with his bicycle past the second entrance into the building, he left the bicycle in the cycle-stand and walked back to the first entrance into the building. He got in through the wide-open collapsible gate and walked up the stairs. It was the same way he'd first gone upstairs sixteen years back for his H.S. course; and today again he was going to the first floor up the same stairs on his first day for the B. Ed course. While climbing up the stairs he remembered to look at the preamble of the Indian constitution painted above the window of the wall at the landing. It was still there but was badly faded.

"I'm back to my dear college once again and I'll have its company for a year," he thought to himself, a pleasure in the deep of his mind played.

B.A., B. Sc girl students of general classes of the morning session were milling around the floors chatting that made a sweet noise. He was feeling kind of unmatched with the environment. He walked up and down the second and third floors aimlessly before he found his classroom. While passing by a bevy of four girls, his eyes fell on the one who looked really pretty and polite; he stopped short, "Are you the students of the B. Ed course here?" he forced himself to ask. In fact, he wasn't smart enough to talk to girls freely for shyness.

"Yes," she replied pleasantly, smiling. It was a little way before the staff room of the college on the first floor veranda.

"I am, too," he answered gratefully, "I'm looking for the classroom. Do you know where it is?"

"It is on the top floor," she said smiling gesturing at the room. Her white teeth looked like precious pearls set up in her mouth. "Thank you," he said and started going past them although he didn't feel like getting away from them. Companion of girls is something to men, always, since humans came to earth. But then Animesh never had a chance for mingling with girls; not even on his own turf nor in school. He studied in a boys' school.

That did it ! Her jolliness, honeyed smile and her beauty touched him beneath as if he had so long been looking for someone like her. He took her into his liking at the first sight.

He walked and wondered if she was engaged which was very much possible. In this era beautiful, nice girls wouldn't be left free so long; specially by the time they have gone through college and university sessions.

Animesh had a pressure from his home to get married right after he'd got the job. Some people had him see a few brides, too, but he wasn't eager about any of them.

At college there would be many girls. He'd had a dormant wish if he found one his way, he would settle it up. This girl seemed to be all right and he wished that she wouldn't slip and fall for anyone else. There must be many like him who'd think the same way.

As he walked up the stairs lazily, he wondered about her name, where she was from and her stream of education. He wished she wouldn't come from Islam or a Brahmin community. There would be a community curb then.

As he got into the classroom, it grated on his nerves to see the benches covered in a thin layer of dust. He felt disgusted for the college authority's carelessness about the poor condition of the classroom. They could have, at least, had them dusted off before the classes started.

"Is this a classroom or something?" He spat out instinctively. Other boys and girls looked at him but they didn't voice a protest in support nor did they show any discontent. He looked around for something like a rag, if left out thereabouts. Just then he remembered of the newspaper in his bag. He took two pages out of the newspaper to lay one on the sitting bench and the other on the high bench. The unknown classmates next to him watched and said, "You did well."

"I had no way other than this. Fortunately, I bought it on the way up here." Animesh replied while laying them on the benches. They too wondered how they would dust their places off. He felt for them for their helplessness. "You can take one from me." He offered.

"Oh, that's very good of you," said the next-seat man in gratefulness. "Thanks."

Animesh gave him one of the unimportant pages. He took it and parted it into two for two of them. They used them for sitting on the seats.

Now he observed them. They looked like good polite people. The first man was Kashinath seemed a bit taller and healthier than Animesh. He wore a checked blue and white full-sleeved shirt and a moustache on his shaved face. The other man, Nirnoy had a light blue vest on, fully-shaved face, widened forehead and light hair on his head with a small baldness visible on his scalp. They got friendly.

There were three rows of benches in the big classroom. Most girls chose the door-side row of benches and they sat there. Animesh talked to Kashinath but his eye went over to the door quite often for the one dearly person he'd just taken into his mind.

At last Animesh saw her getting in with other girls and sitting in the middle of the row towards the door side. In an excuse of looking around the classroom from feigned curiosity, he looked at her and sometimes stole looks at her trying to measure her beauty, her general characteristics, and the like. The more he looked at her, the more he felt interested in her.

In a short time the hall became half-full but none expressed serious discontent over the special layer of dust on the benches. The air felt dusty and damp and smelly, too. It was a post-graduate classroom ! Time ticked on through the noise of their talk.

Soon two professors walked in smartly together straight on to the dais and everybody stood up with a rustling noise to welcome them. The big noise of talking between themselves suddenly went down. They waved their hands to the students to sit down. The younger professor beat at

the chair and the table with the thin register books in an attempt to dust off as much as possible. "The professors themselves have to sit dusting off the chairs and the table, what can we students expect then?" Animesh said out from disgust while watching them do so. They occupied the chairs next to each other. Slowly the younger professor opened the register, took a pen out of his pocket, and got himself ready for the attendance call. They looked at the students pointedly which clearly meant they were drawing attention of the students to cool down.

When the attendance was taken, the pen was put back in his pocket, the registers were closed, the second professor, older than the first one stood up, his forehead was wide, streaks of white hair in his hair showed. He waved his hand again to cool down then he began: "Katwa College welcomes you all to this B. Ed. session cordially. For a year we'll be with you and you with us with reciprocal cooperation, hopes and expectations. You've come from different places and many of you from far-away places and, about the half of you are deputed from different schools. And those who are fresher students, our good wishes go over to you for your future success you've aimed at, and those who are deputed are free from tension anyway. Our good wishes go over to you, too. To many of you it might be a great pleasure to get back the lost old-golden-studentship life once again after many years, I think." He made a short pause. There rose a welcome hum now. It felt Animesh nice as he felt the same way. He chuckled out of a pleasure.

"Anyway, now we're getting introduced with the class. First off, let us introduce ourselves with you. I am R. H. Dutta, and," he looked at the younger professor, who stood up right away, "he is Mr. N. R. Ghoshal," he said. Mr Dutta was senior and older than Mr Ghosal.

They both sat down together. "Here we go from there," Mr. N.R. Ghosal gestured at the young man on the seat by the window farthest right side of the third row. The student stood up waiting for any instruction from the professor. "You tell your name and the place or school you've come from," he instructed.

Students stood up one by one and gave their identity from one side to another forming an 's' that is, from the left to the right hand side. Soon it was time for Animesh's turn. When he stood up, he sneaked a look at her if she was watching. As soon as he finished his identity, she made a gesture questioningly at her friend next to her. Animesh guessed she asked the girl next to her, "What did he say?" And her friend probably said she couldn't hear him either.

"So, it wasn't that she wasn't the least bit interested," Animesh thought and sat down. Almost all girls and boys were interested about the identities of the students. It was quiet natural but the male students made themselves more eager and conscious about the female students' identity. Animesh became aware of Anamika's turn. He watched her stand up and strained his ears for her words to catch unfailingly. Some stupid boy behind him bungled it up by breaking out into a sudden talk and he missed her words. Instinctively the question came out of his mouth: "What's her name, did she say?"

Kashinath sitting next to him broke into a silent smile casting a mischievous look at him. He guessed something. "Anamika Sen or something from Kanchannagar," he said and smiled at him.

"Anamika," Animesh repeated silently in the back his mind. "How sweet her name is!" he thought and turned his head towards her but got back to looking up at the blackboards from guilty-consciousness. "Anamika; Wonderful ! Anyone can fall for her only in her name, and not to speak about her beauty." The name jingled like a sweet chimes in his ears. But the next moment his conscience pricked him. "Oh dear! What's happening right from the first day?" He asked himself guiltily, but he was helpless; he couldn't help, in fact.

Chapter 6

In the B.Ed. course, it seemed that everything performed by a student carried marks, and everyone tired to do at least something. Two days later, there was a class of cultural performance held in the presence of Prof. R. H. Dutta and Prof. N.R. Ghoshal.

Animesh never took part in any stage performance. Naturally, he had great stage fright settled in him which was not so easy to fight off. All the same he thought he would have a go this time, desperately, in need. He had to pluck up courage. Besides, he always wished he could do something in English!

Willing men students and women students did recitations in Bengali, some represented comedies and one guy played the mouth organ. The programme, anyway, got a flow. But with the time going by he started to feel his heart throbbing behind his chest making him think whether he should go in for the performance or not. He had been in two minds about it. Suddenly, he became desperate and stood up just as one guy got off the dais, a legal-size page held in his hand. Prof, R. H. Dutta cued him on to the dais; he walked over casually. A poem was hand-written on it. There was no microphone. His own voice was all that had to reach the end of the big room. He noticed that the sheet of paper trembling in his hand which the students on the first bench could see with awareness. He started reciting his own composition: "To The Supreme God". Half way through he felt his throat choking, his voice trembling although it was masked by the American type of his pronunciation and accent which was influenced by his native English teacher. He swallowed hard. He just got by in a must-go mission. It didn't sound too bad anyway. Walking off the dais he went over to his place and sat down gratefully. Nobody made any comment except Kashinath.

"It's your composition?" he asked and stretched out his hand for the paper.

"Yes," Animesh replied right away giving it to his hand.

After reading it he said, "The theme is good. So, you do some writing, eh?"

"Not really. Rarely, if something takes a form of a thought and only then I have a go."

"Good. Go ahead," he encouraged.

In no time the hot, the palpitation, and the heart's unreasonable throbbing—all died down to normal; he felt that sweat wetted him a little and he looked up at the ceiling fan; it was a little behind him, above his head. He realized what stage fright can do to an unaccustomed stage performer. Suddenly he looked at her: Did she hear me out?" He wondered, trying to read her face.

Chapter 7

He opened the diary for the class routine and found that he had two periods off before the last one. He closed the diary and found it hard finding out what he could do now. Because she wasn't there in the classroom, he felt no pull to stick around the classroom. There weren't anyone he could talk to for he wasn't yet intimated enough with other classmates. Feeling bored, he decided to walk about outside for a while. He rose from his seat, walked out slowly with his bag on his shoulder, strolled along the veranda to the other end and went down the stairs to the ground. There were pairs of boys and girls, or small groups of boys and girls—they were standing by the parapet of the veranda, on the landings of the staircase, under trees and so on. There were chatting, making fun and loafing around. Some were walking hand in hand, or hands on girls' shoulders, or around their waists. It made an ambience like a park in the college, or like a big hotel. It was too much for an educational institute. All the same, he secretly wished he had enjoyed the college-life like them but it dated him. When he turned up at the canteen, he felt a slight shake under his chest; the old memory bobbed up in his mind— "This is the canteen that I came into often enough, sat with my friends and had tea."

There were the same chairs and tables here, the service windows at the same place in the wall. He looked around the square hall and up at the ceiling where the fans were whirling making noises of different kinds. All of them were the same but one thing—the boys and girls out there seemed much more desperate, rude in their appearance and behaviour than at his time. He felt much too uneasy and lonely.

He stood by the food window, asked for a tea, and sat at an empty table near the food window that opened out to the small college-function ground, now it was under water and weeds. He drank it quickly and left the place from uneasiness. Wherever around the college compound he was, there was some memory of the past peeping up in his mind.

He was now passing by the library hall on the first floor when he grabbed a quick look inside the library reading-hall. There were some boys and girls chatting between themselves. He felt hesitated to get in. "This is the library I came into so many times and borrowed books for instant reading there with the yellow card and taking a book home with the green card." He reminisced and kept moving toward the other end. When he was getting up the stairs to the second floor, he heard somebody singing beating at the bench in the classroom. He saw from the door that Kashinath was singing and Nirnoy beating the bench for the tabla. Nirnoy cued him in to join them. He smiled and sat on the bench facing them trying to join in beating at the bench. Then two other guys came and join them. It became a miniature of a function like what his friends Kamalaprasad, Sahadat Ali, Krishnagopal and others used to do in this college sixteen years back. Sahadat and Kamalaprasad both used to sing well. The past situation was back in the same form but what was different was that more than one and a half decades added to his age. Soon the electric bell rang and it was time for the last class.

A few days went by gazing at her secretly. Animesh had been on the lookout for an excuse to speak to Anamika but he didn't find one point strong enough. She had biology but he had Geography for the main method subject. Asking about the subject wouldn't be of help. He wondered what could be a suitable excuse.

The next week he found her in front of him but she was with her friends walking slowly towards the library hall.

"Excuse me," he said suddenly. She looked up at him curiously but her friends cast a hard look at him as if she was the queen and they were her guards and he was an unwanted stranger to kill their queen. He felt a bit discouraged. All the same he got ahead. "Have you bought the books yet?" He asked. She found his question a bit absurd and made a slightly ironical smile, although her smile on her sweet face and uneven teeth didn't look that ironical to him but her friends Mithila, Sana, and Tilli let out some cutting chuckles except Ahalya.

"No," she replied politely enough, "not yet."

Ahalya asked him, "Did you buy?" Her question made the situation a bit easy for him.

Animesh said, "No, not yet. Actually, I don't know whose books would be easier and with short answers."

Ahalya suggested, "You can buy Vedas, all the four papers together, like our old Vedas." It was compared with the four religious Vedas of Hinduism.

"All right," he answered, and not knowing what else to ask, he tried to move forward embarrassed-like. They walked on towards the library and he turned towards the stairs down.

He regretted and cursed himself for pushing himself to speak to her like that, stupidly, and making it a balls-up. He thought of it all the time and wondered how long it would take to make it up.

Chapter 8

Even a trifle could be important and memorable to little people. It happened to Animesh the day he first bought a mobile phone soon after Reliance started its service in Katwa and around. Before, he only saw its adverts in a commercial break during popular Star TV serials—The Bold and The Beautiful and Santabarbara, or Street Legal at Dilip Goenka's House. Animesh used to teach three nephews of Dilip Goenka's in the afternoon and after teaching them, he would watch TV with Dilip in the ground-floor room. Cable TV connection was not much common then. While watching the adverts of Nokia and Motorola mobile sets, he wondered where the technology was going and thought of the lucky people of the Developed World—it was only for them to enjoy its benefits; not for the little people like him. But now India too, got along with the West. In his newly made brick-built house, he looked at his new, grey-blue, Motorola set on the bed and thought, "Who ever thought there would be a mobile phone in this home where we merely scraped by my father's little income; where my father couldn't afford to support me with good enough tuitions for my schooling, but there is a mobile phone today in this home; kind of unbelievably. You can make calls while you're on the move. Such a funny thing it is !" He remembered there was a time in the land-phone era when he'd get scared about talking on the phone wondering how he would dial the number and hold the receiver to his ear and if he would be able to hear from the other side. He wouldn't get into a phone booth unless it was urgent and the booth was empty. He would then phone with the help of the operator. He chuckled to recall those things of those days.

Only years ago a mobile set cost high, call rates were high, you had to pay even for incoming calls. At that time the mobile phone had a dignity. People often would pointedly look the persons using it. The same feeling was true with him too. He would see his Amway Up-lines using them and thought it was possible for them with huge income. He couldn't dare think of a mobile set then. In the first year of his B. Ed course, he had begun to think of owning a mobile. Now came the day—he was in the group of those people using it. It was no surprising that the small ordinary mobile phone made him somehow somewhat proud. Like he himself stole a look at people using mobiles on the train or anywhere those days, so did he at people—if they were noticing him the same way when he was using it. He, however, had hardly anyone to talk to on the phone except for his Up-line persons of Amway. Still he bought it, kind of hurriedly, thinking about Anamika—he'd already taken a shine to her. What he expected most, was that she would certainly own a mobile phone soon and he would have some chances or pretexts to talk to her. He kept waiting for that day.

Chapter 9

Animesh was in the canteen sitting quietly thinking things over while drinking tea. Suddenly he heard a thunder rumble in the sky. He thought he shouldn't get stuck here in the rain. So, he downed the tea to the dregs just in a few gulps and came out of the canteen.

He looked up at the sky and saw bluish grey rain-clouds up in the eastern sky. The base of the clouds looked fader and fragile that indicated it was coming up shedding rain. No sooner than he thought of it, it started dripping in large drops. He walked fast up to the main building without taking his umbrella out of his bag. He didn't want to have it wetted to cross the little way up to the building. The rain began to fall heavily and he had to run up to the second entrance of the main building. He walked up the stairs to the first floor. He got wet a little and tried to wipe his hair and his hands with the handkerchief looking out at the rain. It was raining hard by now. He enjoyed watching it for a short while.

He slowly walked along the long veranda and then up the stairs to the second floor at the other side still watching the rain on the move. From the door of his classroom, he could hear a melodious chorus song of Rabidranath coming from the room next to his classroom. It was the "Soghono Gohono Ratri Jhorichhe Shraban Dhara" suitable for the rainy season. Music was something he was really fond of. From the door he looked in and stopped short; there was a bunch of big kids. His eye fell on Anamika first, then on Kashinath, Sangita, Ahalya and Utpal. They were around the table forming a half circle. On the table was the harmonium. Utpal was playing the tabla.

He walked into the room, kind of hesitantly and smiled at Kashinath as he met Animesh's eyes and he smiled back. He kept watching them singing; in fact, watching her singing. His eager eyes often fell on Anamika's long beautiful fingers flicking skillfully across the harmonium buttons, and on her teeth out of her wonderfully moving lips. He felt himself like an unwanted person in the singing choir but still he couldn't tear himself away from the room. He regretfully thought to himself: "If I'd learnt singing for just one year and a half like Kashinath had, I could have taken a part in this nice programme today. I had enough time in Burdwan since I had the job." Unfortunately, learning to sing didn't come to his lot. For a while his memory ran back to his childhood when he'd been reading in class eight. His father had been asked by the school office to get his book-grant money for two years; 180 rupees. After receiving the money from the office, he had been walking for home behind his father down the concrete road by the boundary wall of the school. Near the end of the boundary wall he'd plucked up guts and said out, "Father?"

Sudhinra replied right away without turning his face, "Yes?"

"Will you buy me a harmonium with this money? I will learn singing." He fondly demanded.

"Singing! He said surprised, "Hmhh?!" He snapped sarcastically. "There's no use of learning to sing." He turned down his request nastily. Belonging to a poor family, he knew it was like crying for the moon. All the same he'd ventured. He kept walking behind him with a heavy heart. Since then he never pronounced his wish ever again. He just nurtured this idea that singing wouldn't be in reality in this life. He used to listen and croon to himself. That was all. Whenever the tune of a harmonium came to his ears from a house on the way, it gave a stir to his heart and felt an urge to stop and listen for a while stopping there. It made him sad and release a sigh of despair.

The song went to an end, they talked about the mislead parts of the tunes. Animesh became conscious of it. "You too can sing well enough," said Kashinath looking at him. "Come on and take part in it." It was tempting enough for him to be asked in singing. "But I don't know the song in full," he said hesitantly. In fact, he really felt tempted to take part in it in spite of being scared about the stage for he never ever sang in his open voice, and not to speak of singing on the stage. "Then I need the lyrics." He implied his acceptance of the great offer. At least he would be able to stay with the bunch, say, with her, and watch her and his luck might be favourable to get closer to her. One thing he noticed subtly that she neither opined against nor in favour of him.

"Here it is. You can copy it down later. Come on. Go to it."

Ahalya turned the copybook a little towards him and moved over slightly to make room for him. He moved over next to Ahalya. Now he sweated a bit more from tension. He found it getting well enough as he sang with them twice. With happiness in his mind on his way back, he bought a cassette of that song in an album by Hemanta Mukherjee and played it back many times over at home to make it come as best as he could.

During the days of rehearsal in college he took her more deeply into his heart as a result of stolen gazes at her frequently.

He had been looking to have a chance to talk to her but he had no chance at all. Only while she was among themselves in the rehearsal, he was able to ask her one or two unmatched questions about her singing. She, however, answered them smilingly but she didn't ask anything back about him which would have felt him encouraging. The compositions of her lips and eyes naturally created smiley expressions.

Near the final day of the rehearsal, he was kind of worried because he couldn't speak to her a bit personally yet. Although he planned to speak to her kind of desperately, but it started to grow tension in his heart.

Today he saw her walking out of the rehearsal room down the stairs talking with Ahalya. He followed them. At the landing of the stairs he thought he would speak but he couldn't. He followed them till the ground and then to let them walk farther ahead of him, he stopped short by the flower garden before the main entrance gate and pretended to look into his bag for something. By the time they were out of the gate and took a right turn towards Matangini Girls' Hostel women's hostel. He walked fast to catch them up before they got in through the small grill-gate of the hostel. He felt an urge to call her from the back and he did. He stupidly called, "Anamika?"

She obviously felt it unexpected. She turned around to look back; her hand was on the latch on the top of the grill-gate. Behind her was Ahalya. Her surprised look left him in uneasiness and a feeling of guilt. "Oh dear! It is damn hard to decide how I should represent what I actually wanted to tell her." He thought regretfully. The heart's throbbing was felt under his chest. "I wanted to talk to you about something," he quickly said out with guts.

"Tell me," she said coldly. Ahalya looked eagerly to listen with a faint chuckle.

"No, not now," he said, "Tell you later, individually."

"How important is it that you need to tell me and that too, individually?" She asked. Her seriousness got him scared. He felt like being vanished right away.

"No, it's not so much of that," he said, trying to make it light and casual.

He didn't see her react to it in any way. She turned and gravely opened the gate and went in. He turned back and shook his head from regret and walked up to the gate. His bad luck was also at his step. Trishan had watched him. "Got the green signal?" he asked smiling mischievously at him.

"Green signal?" He countered, but fearfully. "Was this guy following me?!" He wondered.

"Don't you try to hide it from me," Trishan warned mockingly. "I watched you."

He smiled. "I didn't tell her anything. I just told her I wanted to talk, later."

"Any way, if so, don't get late. She might be somebody else's," he suggested with a mixture of latent warning. Animesh wondered if she was in Trishan's liking as well because he was smarter, more handsome, and proper to the age-match. It was possible for a few others, too, to lean to her as well. Anxiety began to chase him now. He didn't see the least encouragement in her of learning about what he'd wanted to tell her.

A few days went by. The rehearsal course was over. It was the Teachers' Day; the day for their performance in the function. He brought in more humiliation for himself that day. The chorus team was set after the preliminary programs like the offering of homage flowers to the image of Dr. Radha-krishnan, the inaugurating song, and then their chorus.

The men stood behind the microphone wearing white churidar Panjabi shirt. He borrowed it from his friend, Tushar. He felt a bit uneasy shyness after he had worn them in college because he had never used them before. It felt him a little uneasy. On the other hand, he'd never had any experience of singing on the stage before. While singing he happened to think he was a bit farther from the microphone and his voice wasn't caught right. He leant forward closer to the microphone which made his voice too loud and unmatched to the other singers'. Prof. N.R. Ghosal told the operator to turn down the volume of the sound-box to sound better. This was something that got him and he felt embarrassed, very much. The sound from the chorus voice was enough for the big classroom though. Anamika and others sang it naturally. He regretted for his bad performance. This embarrassing failure failed him once again to think of telling her what he had wanted to speak. He wanted to wait a few days till the thorn of uneasiness weakened or went down.

Chapter 10

Animesh didn't realize how time had gone by. In the mean time the test exams were performed. The results were not good. So, he was in concern. Today they, the three pals— Animesh, Kashinath and Nirnoy were wandering about the college compound. At last they drifted into the canteen.

The canteen was not crowded today. Arnab and Abhik had already been there sitting face to face by the window just in front of the service counter. Arnab smiled and called, "Come on over here, Animesh." Animesh smiled back and nodded for his okay and moved over to the service counter in front of Arnab's table. Nirnoy and Kashinath were behind him. "Three teas please," he said to the service boy and remembered to offer Arnab tea, "Five teas," he turned to Arnab right away. "Arnab, have tea with us, will you?"

"No, no, you get yours," he objected with a brief smile. "Ours have already been ordered for and will right be down."

"Okay, then," he said, and turned to the boy again with the correction, "Not five, three teas for us."

"Like cookies?" he asked turning to Kashinath. "No cookies, only tea," he replied.

Animesh went over to Arnab and called them over to sit. Nirnoy drew up another table to join it to the other, and Kashinath got two chairs. He sat next to Arnab. Kashinath, and Nirnoy sat next to Abhik. They formed an oval-sitting tea-chat around the rectangular table.

"So, how are things?" Arnab asked Animesh, his hands lying across the table.

"Mustn't grumble, anyway," Animesh replied. "We can't stop it or propel it our way."

The tea boy called over for the tea. Abhik got two for them and Nirnoy got three for themselves. The teacup was bigger than usual. The earthen cup smelled of burnt clay and ash. It was usual. That was its specification of tea in earthen cups. The slurps went for a while when a few words were spoken. When it was about to be over, Abhik's eyes looked over them at the door behind.

Nirala was there. She was his girl friend. He gulped down the rest of the tea quickly. "Be seated, you guys. I'll be going," Abhik said and stood up and went out.

Animesh felt easier now. He wasn't close with that guy because he thought him to be a bit biased-friendly to specific guys.

Arnab noticing Animesh's face became suddenly curious, and asked, "Are you alright? Your health?"

"Yes, my health is alright but I'm worried about the exam results. It's worse than ever." Animesh replied.

"Why worry?" Arnab asked reproachfully. "Everybody did badly in this term; almost all deputed ones. Mine is even worse," he consoled. Kashinnath and Nirnoy also agreed with him. "Yes, our results are bad, too." But he was worried not just about the result, but more about Anamika. The time had flown by leaving him in a trance of the first ever love in his life that he couldn't tell. That was what put an effect on his exams. On the other hand his memory worsened from ten years' sustained tension, and unsuccessfully running after an opportunity abroad and being unemployed during the years. The tensed, restive brain was nearly destroyed.

"Did you buy the books?" Animesh asked.

""Books?" Nirnoy cut in, "Why Books? They won't help now. Try to get some old notes from somebody."

"But I don't know anybody I can ask for notes," he said hopelessly. "Who am I gonna ask for them?"

"Don't worry. I have friends to get them from. Let me get them and I'll give you to get them xeroxed," Arnab reassured him.

"Thank you, friend?" Animesh said out of comfort.

Suddenly a familiar voice cried, "Hey, you guys here?"

They all looked back at the door. Trisan and Anuradha walked in and over to the farthest corner of the hall by the window round the corner. Animesh could guess that the pair sought comparatively lonelier place to stay away from this bunch.

Arnab raised his hand, "Everything's okay?"

"Yes, all is okay." Trishan called his reply in courtesy and sat down at the table there.

"Yeah, they are all right. They're making best use of the brief student's life," Arnab said laughing.

"Will their love last in the end? Or is it just for using one another for the study material?" Kashinath asked casually.

"Who knows?" Arnab answered doubtfully. "There go a number of love affairs in every B. Ed. session but about three or four get matured to marriage." He spilled out the collected information.

Here Anamika came into Animesh's mind and he became thoughtful. He thought if someone else would snatch his doll away before he succeeded. In the meantime, however, many students of the class knew about his weakness for her but he was still in the drawback that he hadn't had any reply yet to his message he'd sent to her. He wondered if his message was delivered or not.

"Hey, mister, you seemed to be lost in thought." Kashinath said waving his hand before Animesh's eyes.

"No, nothing," he replied startled.

"What about your Anamika?" Kashinath demanded.

Asking or telling him about Anamika gave him sort pleasure and he liked it.

"Who knows? I ain't seen her?" He replied casually.

"Who knows!" Nirnoy mimicked in a surprised tone looking at his face with a broad smile, his eyes bulged.

"Your doll, you won't keep her updates, then who else will?" Nirnoy burst out and they all laughed.

Kashinath added to it, "You don't love her?"

"Yes, I do love her. Certainly," He confessed honestly.

"Then? What's wrong?" Kashinath and Nirnoy asked together.

"To love and being loved is not easy for everybody," Arnab said wisely.

"I love her but I don't know if she feels a thing about me." With a pause he added, "I sent her messages but I haven't got any reply yet." He explained ruefully.

"Be bold and be quick, Mister, if you want your beloved bird to be yours, or else," Kashinath paused for a moment and everybody looked at his face eagerly, when Nirnoy blurted out picking the thread "or else, your bird will sit in another nest." It suggested another indirect warning that gave a stir to his heart.

"Tell me, then, I will help you. I will tell her," Nirnoy demanded.

"Of course, I will you in need," Animesh told him, "But let me have a go myself first."

"Go ahead," he encouraged, "but don't be late."

"But, above all, you believe it or not," Arnab opened his mouth again and paused shortly, "Love is a thing that completely depends on your favourable star sign. Observe this on people—you will see beautiful girls, educated women run after guys who are undereducated, ugly looking and skinny, and loafers while many gentlemen with good qualities, or wealth can't find one to be in love with. I understood it with myself."

"Yes, this is very right," Nirnoy said right away with a big smile. "The others who are successful without that star sign, they can be too desperate in worshipping or in nagging at girls and in the continued nagging or worshipping they break down at a point of time and slip into an affairs which would turn their lives sour someday sooner, and later into a disaster."

"In all truth," Kashinath said, "I would say women are no intelligent. They can't make a difference between what is constructive and what is destructive. That's why they fall into trouble later on." They all agreed to that. Arnab said, "Zodiac sign was one thing that mattered to every section of one's life; one's loss or gain, or prosperity, whatever." I believe it. The admitted it by nodding. Animesh thought fearfully, "Where will my fortune take me to?"

Chapter 11

Time seemed to be the fasted thing in the world. Animesh had been feeling bad right from weeks before, whenever the uneasy thought of the up-coming puja vacation came into his mind. Today was the last day for the month-long vacation. He wouldn't be able to see Anamika even for once in the long vacation. He couldn't take it easy because his affair was yet to be thick enough so as to be in touch with her the other way. The other men or women who had been thick enough would be in touch right, but him? He asked himself. So, he was restive.

Two periods of class were held so far and another was expected from Sindhu sir, who would give class-notes for English. By the time they roamed around, sat around, and loafed around with teacups in hand in the canteen hall and elsewhere; they chatted in the classroom, Kashinath sang as usual, Animesh sang along with him and Nirnoy tapped his fingers on the high bench for the tabla substitute. Arnab, Jewel and Utpal joined later. Sometime later there came a girls' bunch and sat face to face on their usual place in the classroom and talked funny things that burst with their occasional giggles. Anamika wasn't in the bunch. Feeling tempted the boys' bunch went over to them and their jokes stopped right away. They demanded of Arnab to tell jokes. He was the man of jokes. He told two jokes and they almost split their sides laughing.

They all then exchanged their contact numbers to speak in need during the vacation. Those who had their mobile contact numbers, they shared their numbers and those with land phone numbers shared theirs, too. "It feels me bad to think we won't see one another for a long month," said Arnab. Kashinath and Nirnoy agreed with him, "Certainly, they said.

"Yes, I'll be missing you, too, very much," Animesh said sadly and sighed out but he knew who he would be missing so much. "Anamika," he recited her name in his mind. "Why couldn't I reach you yet?" The name sent him a cold blow into his heart and shook it—he wished he'd had her number. Unfortunately, she didn't have a mobile phone yet, but she had a land phone number, which was not so easy to get. Today he felt like watching her more than ever. His mind was running after her. The thought made him more restive now. But where was she?

Suddenly he got up from his seat. It looked odd to their eyes. They looked up at him curiously. "To toilet," he answered before they had a chance to ask. "I'll be right back." So saying he got out and lost himself for her.

As she got down the stairs from the second floor (in British English) to the first floor, he stopped short. His eyes caught sight of Anamika on the veranda on the other side of the second floor with her companions. "There she is! The beauty queen!" he thought and hurried back onto the second floor and stood by the parapet with a slanted line of proper distance opposite from them.

He was feasting his eyes on her; his eyes seemed to have been locked on her beautiful face as she was chatting with her friends, her hand resting on the parapet. Sangita was on her right, and on her left were Sana and Tilli whom Animesh never liked at all, not because he had words with them; for no reason in particular but still he happened to get an irritation to see them. There are some people who you never met before; all the same their appearance and dress make you feel disgust for them even not knowing why. Those two girls looked rude, wore mostly in grey or black mourning-kind-of dress, and also were introvert and malicious.

Abruptly it clicked in his mind that his continuous look might send a bad message to them. He tore his eyes away to other directions, but for a moment only, the gaze soon got back by her attraction, and several times it happened. One of the friends of hers poked at her side nodding her head at Anamika then quickly over at Animesh mischievously smiling and saying something. The other two girls followed her indication and looked over at him and turned to themselves and smiled, then laughed, and they all looked over at him again and turned to themselves. He felt they reported to her of his gaze at her. Feeling shy Anamika threw her hand lightly at her in denial. Animesh observed all these like a keen look of an egale.

He chuckled to himself and just as he turned around to leave, Ahalya was there behind him watching him sneakily and smiling. Animesh didn't know when she came behind him on her way down. He felt embarrassed and smiled back at her shyly.

"It's all right," she slightly leant forward and said in a suppressed voice. "It happens in real love." Now she spoke normally. "I understand how much you're gone on her, Animesh-da." Her favourable worlds sounded sweet and encouraging to him.

"But you didn't get me any positive news yet. Isn't it your failure, Ahalya?" He asked accusingly.

"It's my failure, of course. I confess," she replied smiling. "She doesn't make things clear—'yes'-or-'no'—nothing."

"Could she be in love with anybody in the college?" He asked. "Do you have any idea?"

She shook her head. "No, with none in here, sure," she answered. He breathed out happiness forcibly. "That's fine," he said. It comforted him greatly.

"But I don't know if with anyone else, elsewhere. I think she isn't, or else we must have got some indication," she explained. Animesh wished she wouldn't be engaged with anyone else.

"They are probably watching you complainingly," Ahalya said seriously.

"Yeah, I feel it the same way. Let's go." They moved out of the spot and split away on their own different way. Animesh feeling hard to tear himself away stole a look at her a few more times down the stairs towards the ground floor.

The last day of college before the vacation was over. He got buried in sadness with her name in the deep of his heart.

Chapter 12

There were two puja pandals of the youth clubs near Animesh's house from where loudspeaker's sound could reach him at home. Right from the dawn Bengali soft songs were coming through the air from the pandals. Durga Puja was the best and biggest religious festival to the Bengalis running for five consecutive days. This time they would get themselves new clothes, buy new clothes for their folks, and also for their relatives. Even the poorest parents would try to buy their children new clothes. Popular tailors would get busier from two months before and wouldn't want to take new orders three weeks before the Puja.

At his childhood, Animesh enjoyed the festival very much with immense pleasure wearing new clothes walking out to visit Durga idols with his local friends all the way for more or less twelve kilometers down to the levee along the river side in the low land area and then on the up-land around his small town and by the railway station and then back home making a big circle of the route.

After he'd passed out from college, his pleasure started to be less and less with him; he didn't feel excited about the any festivals. He didn't put on his new clothes made for the festival. His father would express discontent over this. When his father asked, "Why didn't you put on your new clothes on this puja day?" He would say, "Wearing new clothes is most appropriate for kids, Dad. I'm no longer a kid." He tried to reason out. In fact, he felt kind of shy in wearing new clothes on these days at his unemployed period. And that practice still went on even after he'd had this plumb job of a high school teacher's. Thus, it had been a number of years since he didn't go out looking around idols in any festivals. Instead, he spent the evenings loafing around with his English guru and English mates at their usual places they used to sit around. They all were of his mind, wouldn't like the crowds, or noise.

If talking about this year, there is a matter of a special thing. Only a few days passed away since the vacation started, in the mean time, he started gasping for college. He felt it was ages since he saw her face. He bore her name in his heart and in his work from time to time, the name bobbed up and gave a jerk under his chest. So, he wanted to spend the time idly at home sitting around, reading and making notes for the final exams.

It was the Maha Ashtamee Day. Animesh woke up from pain in the abdomen which seemed to burst. The abdomen swelled hard from urine in the bladder. And he had to go to the toilet. He looked up at the clock with bleary eyes on the wall. It was nearly four o'clock. He was back to bed. The early morning of the old autumn made the air of the room cooler through the open windows to the pond. He turned the ceiling fan down; still he felt cold and drew the bed sheet over his body up to his chest and lay quite thinking with his closed sleepy eyes. He fell asleep again—

The canteen was unusually empty. They chose a table in front of the service counter by the windows that opened out to a small open field to the west. It was soggy and full of long grass. They were sitting face to face eating omelettes from the white plates on the table.

"Did you ever fall for anybody?" Animesh asked her as he put his fork up towards his mouth with a cut-piece of omelette speared on it.

"No, never," she answered while eating her omelette.

"And you?" Anamika asked him casting a curious look at him.

"No, not before," he replied and speared another piece from the plate. "Now I did," he said and put the piece into his mouth. "I remember the very first day on the first-floor veranda when I saw you answer to my question with a marvelous smile. I liked you right at that moment. By and by, your good appearance, your personality, and the looks of intelligence in you influenced me deeply." He went on. She listened to him looking at his face, sort of distrust in her expression, but with a mischievous chuckle, her fork poised over her plate.

"And with days going by, I knew more of you and I got more interested in you," Animesh continued.

She smiled and put in another piece into her mouth, "You ain't eating, finish it while it's warm," she said. Animesh looked down at his plate and put another piece into his mouth.

"I understood my liking was reasonable which in no time turned into love, the true love, I would say." She chuckled, her lips pressed as if to hold it back. She rightly guessed he was a bit too emotional. She said, "You seem to be a simple guy."

Animesh smiled. "May be, or maybe not. Who knows? But what I know is I speak out the way I feel things." He took another piece of omellete up on the fork and into his mouth.

"Anyway, I told you about my feeling. What is your feeling towards me?"

She felt shy here, "nothing," she replied evasively.

"Not just 'nothing', baby. Nothing can't happen for nothing. Or else you wouldn't be here and neither would I be with you."

She smiled shyly. "Women can't express emotional feeling as easily as men," he thought.

"Come on; tell," he insisted, "One hand can't clap for two, can it?" Animesh felt he heard faint sounds of knocks and calls from behind him at the canteen door.

"Okay, let me tell, ..."

There was a loud knock on the door and he woke up. He heard his mother call, "Get up, it's near seven o'clock."

"Oh, shit! It's bungled up," he breathed out automatically and felt irritated at his mother's untimely call. Right away he understood the actual thing. He looked out with his half-opened eyes across the foot of the bedstead through the big open window; the wide daylight played over the pond. "The sun must have climbed quite above in the east," he thought. He lay quiet on the bed for sometime thinking and enjoying it. The whole day went by happily as it bobbed up in his mind quite often and went on for a few days. Whenever he reminisced of it since that day, he asked himself, "Did it mean anything significant for the reality tomorrow?" He became more restive for the college to open and see her. He was waiting for the excursion tour after the vacation expecting her in the group of the tour.

Chapter 13

November was the pre-winter season. The day was breaking with faint grey light over in the east as they got down bleary eyed from the big tourist bus. They had been on an excursion tour to Rajgir in Bihar state. It was a famous place for Lord Buddha. Animesh felt it was a lot colder in Rajgir than in his plain-land district and wished he would finish the tour without any health trouble and get back home alright. He couldn't figure out for the warm clothes in a hilly, plateau state of Bihar.

They checked in a hotel here. They went for the morning calls of nature. The girls were provided with two big rooms and the men with another two rooms. Having the morning tea first and a while later, the breakfast on snacks, they got out to look around. They visited the Vishwa Shanti Stupa. It was a very big white temple of Lord Buddha. Animesh was enchanted to see the magnificent sculptural works of the temple and beautifully shaped gardens of well-trimmed hedges at the front and around the temple.

Inside the temple, he sat on the white marble floor along with them in front of the big golden idol of Lord Buddha and prayed with his hands joined together, his head slightly down. Everybody prayed for their own expectations, and Animesh was no exception. He still couldn't shake off his long-cherished dream of an emigration abroad. But here he couldn't think of anything else other than 'her'. He prayed for the dream he had a month ago come true.

He missed her so much here. He thought she would be at the tour, but she wasn't. He'd expected to see her giggling, laughing and enjoying the beauty of these places. He might have had an opportunity to speak to her a bit freely. But she didn't come. He let out a deep sigh.

Suddenly it clicked in his heart that he was thinking of all these worldly thoughts. Now his mind began to freshen up recalling the wrongs he had done so far.

So long as you stay in a holy religious place, you would have your mind changed in the ambience of God and Goddess—the feeling of sin and virtue would bob up in the core of your mind and filter your mind afresh. Regrets, compunctions and confessions—all would rise in the deep of the heart. That would be the greatness of the religious places. He prayed to Lord Buddha to forgive him for the wrongs he had done so long. But he didn't have enough power to think if his running after Anamika was any wrong.

From here they went to ride the ropeway. Rajgir Rope Way was the most attractive spot of the tour. The hill-cars carried them up the zigzag hill-cut way to the cable car station. Many of the girls got scared to see the cable car hanging from the cable and moving up into the distance in the void and jibbed at riding. Animesh too, first got a bit scared but soon he won the fright. He watched keenly how the people got on the car while it was on the slow move because it wouldn't stop.

They stood in a queue. When the attendant put down the iron rod before him and locked it walking along with the car a little way on the platform, and the car went past the platform, his eyes went down. It was all empty under his feet. It gave him a sudden startle from eeriness. He felt a slight quiver to his feet and a mixed peculiar feeling of fear and thrilling that went away soon as he looked straight and around. As the cable cars climbed up and up towards the still higher hill in the thin layer of smog, the cars far off looked to him like a flock of big birds flying one behind anther. He looked around over the lush green jungle sporadically infested with colourful flowers.

The first time ever he was on the cable car. He was so excited that he felt like shouting joyously to let out his feeling. Instead, he exclaimed, "Wow! How marvellous!"

Here he remembered Anamika again—if she had been here today what she would have done now, how she would enjoy it. The thought made him cool and expressionless. He could imagine she was in the car right behind him shouting in joy with her friends. In his thought, he really turned his head back. It was then Danesh Sinha called him over.

"Hey man, getting scared?"

Animesh didn't reply. Again he called, "Hey, are you scared? How are you enjoying it?"

"Oh no. Not getting scared." Animesh's reply spread out in the air. "I'm enjoying it, real nice."

"Are you scared?" He called emphatically.

"No, not me either," Danesh shouted his reply. "I like it very much. It's a new kind thrilling, isn't it?"

"Yes. But I'm not satisfied. The length should have been longer up to that hill over the thicker jungle," Animesh shouted back gesturing at the faraway taller hill.

"Next time you can." Danesh shouted.

On that day, the many places he visited including the Nalanda debris, he missed her very much.

From the next morning he started sneezing a lot with a runny nose and coughing lightly, and by and by the coughing turned nasty which left him in uneasiness. Cold had caught him badly. On stepping out of the bus the previous day, he had felt it. A half sweater, a scarf, a full-sleeved shirt and shoes were not enough in that plateau's young winter. He bought a wrapper from a local shop at Nalanda which helped him a little but not enough. He wrapped himself up in it all the while in the bus, but still the stubborn cold pierced into his flesh. All the way home he coughed badly so often that he felt guilty of his bad cough disturbing the others in their sleeping attempt. It made him badly sick from rib-splitting coughing. For a moment he thought that it was better that Anamika didn't come. Or else, he would have been in greater embarrassment.

Chapter 14

By mid 1991 when Animesh had been unemployed for about four years after he had graduated from Katwa College and he was still looking for a job, some guy had proposed his father to get his son married to their girl with a promise that they would secure him a government job after marriage but Animesh turn down the offers. He had said, "It'll be humiliating for my self-dignity. The wife will prick me any time that her father established me. Let me try myself for some time more, and then I'll if I have to."

Sudhindra finding his words reasonable didn't try to convince him. Animesh, however, was not trying all out for a job like other kids on the turf did. Ashim got a job in the LIC, his brother got one in Durgapur Steel Plant in less than two years. Ashim encouraged him to work hard and, if necessary, to get some coaching as well, but Animesh had been engulfed by an addiction of learning Oxford English with a new dream grown up in him—to go abroad and be settled. A new confidence had grown in him that he had learnt enough English of international standard and he wouldn't have to be in trouble at work in foreign land or turn back home to his native land for want of English. It was this dream that had held him back from being serious about a job or accepting any marriage offer for a decade. Precious time had gone by without success in his determined aim. At last he understood he had been running about the vast open field with no way at all, he would have to get on the road first, that is, to get a job at any cost and this was the job that he obtained at last.

This evening Animesh was at Bapi's house. Bapi lived in Durgapur at his work place from many years before, in the mid 90s. And Animesh started living in Burdwan after he'd had a teacher's job about five years later than Bapi. Animesh would visit this house once a week or still less to see them.

He sat on the bed of the bedroom as usual for there wasn't a drawing room in that house that they lived in on rent for decades. After some casual talk while cutting vegetables sitting on the floor, Bapi's elder sister, Putul said, "Hey, what about your marriage?" She didn't take her eyes from the cutting tool. "Did you find a bride yet?" Animesh was kind of unprepared for this question. "Marriage?" he asked back hesitantly to find an answer. In fact, he was tired of answering these questions so many times to so many people.

"Yes, your marriage," she said looking up at him. She was slim and very beautiful, with her slightly wavy hair, and a sharp nose.

"No, didi," he replied weakly, "Trying to..."

"When else will you marry? Have you thought you've already been late enough?"

Her mother joined the topic. "Get married, Animesh, or else, you won't have time to raise your children, honey. You can't realize it now." She said making tea in the kitchen. "Should I find you one? I have news of a bride, a good one, from a good family."

How could he ever tell the truth why he is not trying to get married? It was embarrassing to tell that he fell in 'deep love' with Anamika in college but one-sided love. That's why he couldn't declare boldly. He didn't know what will happened to it in the end. He gulped down and said,

"The house has just been completed. Soon I'll settle it up, Auntie. For fear of facing more questions about this matter, he wanted to leave but they didn't let him go without having tea.

So, he waited for tea and heaved a sigh of concern. How will he ever succeed!

Chapter 15

The week-long Charismas vacation followed by the New Year's Day holiday was over. College reopened. Animesh felt happy to think that he could see her and perform the planned jobs to succeed in wining her heart. But college was not as lively as it had been before the vacation. It was usual after each vacation. It seemed that the college just woke up from a slumber whose effect was yet to go.

He got into the classroom lazily and found a few students sitting, a few others standing sporadically across the room chatting. The benches had a thin layer of dust as usual that grated on his nerves. The room smelled damp and cold. Complaints didn't do any good. He had to dust off his seat himself again with something like he'd done six months before. Animesh's eyes often went to the open door looking forward to seeing her. He'd wanted to give her a New Year's Greeting Card himself. But she was not in sight yet.

One by one they got in and occupied their chosen seats in the classroom and there was a patter of beating at the benches with folded newspaper or exercise books. Arnab, Kashinath, Nirnoy, Jewel, Danesh, Trishan—all came in and greeted him with 'Happy New Year'. He greeted them with the same. He greeted Ahalya, Sangita, Debsmita, Shrinika as he met them; and also a few others who he was easy with. But the one he was crazy for was not up yet.

After the first period of class had been over, Animesh went out with his bag on his shoulder. He was back from eating the breakfast and then he did another class. At last he saw her when she was going over to the other classroom for her method subject. He saw her walking ahead of him down the veranda of the second floor with Ahalya, Sana and Tilli. It gave a sudden quiver to his heart. He had the palpitation. He couldn't tell her anything. There were the two villains with her. He steered back and went out again and strolled around the canteen, then down the first floor of the veranda, and again down by the front garden path for a while, then he went out through the gate aimlessly with sadness of failure. He jolted his head regretfully. "This job is not for me," he thought. He made up his mind that he'd have Ahalya send it over to her.

After he had tea at the tea kiosk a little way behind the college, he was walking back into the classroom lazily. He kept on thinking how he could give the card to her.

From a little distance he saw Ahalya walking from her hostel towards the gate into the college building. He walked fast to catch up with her before she got in through the gate.

"Ahalya?" He called her from the back at the gate before she crossed it. She stopped short and turned her head to the call. "Just a minute," he raised his hand to her. She had Mithila, and Tilli with her. She asked them to move ahead.

He walked over to her. She guessed from the tone of the call that he had something in his mind.

His palpitation had a boost. "What's up, Animesh-da?" she asked looking up at him curiously. 'Da' is used with man's name for 'dada' meaning 'elder brother' in Bengali. There was a suppressed chuckle on her lips.

"Will you do me a favour, please?" he said hesitantly.

"Why not, if it goes with me?" She reassured him plainly. "What favour?" She demanded softly.

"You'll have to reach my greeting card to her, please." His hand gestured quickly at his bag.

"Ahalya was silent for a moment thinking while Animesh looked at her face waiting for her answer.

"Can't you give it to her yourself?" She asked mockingly smiling as if it was a casual thing.

"Isn't it better if you give it to her yourself?" She asked suggestively, or rather wanting to avoid it.

"It won't be right," he replied, "Time hasn't come yet, and you know it." He answered.

"Okay," she agreed half willingly, "if I have to."

"Please, do it for me?" He opened the bag and took out a folded yellow polythene carrier bag that couldn't be seen through. He took out the envelope with Anamika's name written in style in fat letters on it and handed it to her.

Then he took out another envelope, her name written in the same style. "This one's for you," he said and smiled. She took it smiling with him. "Thank you," she said. "Okay, I'll give hers to her."

"Put 'em in this poly bag and then in your bag," he said softly. He didn't want anyone of her friends to see it and be curious about it.

Ahalya walked ahead and up the stairs. Animesh followed her down the same way but rather slowly with a distance, his head slightly bent.

Now with the time going by, concern began to rise and spread out and it began to worry him by and by; a fear of scandal. "Did I do right?" He wondered. "In the months gone by things didn't come off satisfactorily."

A timid guy would be scared at every step in his life and fail and remorse then. He thought, "How will she take it? How will she react? Will she accept it? Or will she make a chaos over it?

If the scandal would be chalked on the walls, on the posters! It would be a humiliating gossip of the college. Many kids were at college from my area. It would be humiliating for me." This imagined apprehension bobbed up in his timid sensitive mind because he was no longer merely a student at this college but a teacher from a high school. Teachers in the society were socially isolated from the rest of the crowd—they shouldn't have any other feelings like people of other walks of professions.

A stone thrown out of the hand couldn't be brought back or stopped. His thought fought over this matter in two ways. His mind said it shouldn't have been sent, but his heart's trend was in favour, or else, he would have to forget her forever. That's what he could never do. He felt she was pulling him like a strong magnet. So, risking was the only way to it—'No risk, no gain,' the proverb came in support to him.

Chapter 16

The next day it ran on everyone's lips of most of the girls that Animesh had given Anamika a New Year's greetings card. It was not a scandal but a thing nice to talk about. Those who were not in a friendly term with him gave him a chuckle on seeing him with a mischievous look; some of the friendly ones just asked him personally in order to know the truth of the rumour. He answered them as best as he could. At first, Animesh got confused how it went over with them and guessed that some girl known must have seen Animesh give something like a letter to Ahalya and she pried into it trickily.

What Animesh had feared came true. He asked himself apprehensively what more would come next. He thought of observing Anamika to guess any reaction from reading her face but she didn't come today. So, his concern held on.

Another day passed away in concern with no trace of Anamika in the college. Her two days' absence made him more concerned. "Maybe she had been offended very much. And that's why she didn't come to college two days in a row," he thought to himself anxiously. He was getting scared if she was going to complain to the principal against him. While thinking he took his bicycle out of the cycle-shade when his eyes fell on Trishan looking up at him. Animesh walked up to him with his bicycle looking at Trishan.

"Is it true what I hear, Animesh?" Trishan asked plainly. He noticed his mischievous smile.

"Animesh pretended that he didn't understand the question but it shook him inwardly.

"What did you hear, friend?" he asked. It sounded weak enough although he tried to speak casually.

"You sent Anamika a letter or something?" he asked.

"But I ask who told you this important news?" he asked.

"Girls were talking about something like this and then it was clear to me," he replied smiling.

Animesh nodded, "I see," he breathed out and stayed silent for a moment. He thought he ought to dispel any wrong idea out of Trishan that he'd heard.

"No letter it was, actually," Animesh answered convincingly with a casual tone. Trishan waited to hear the next words more curiously.

"It was a greeting card for the New Year's."

"Only a greeting card?" Trishan asked surprised, "Why didn't you send a letter as well with your pent up feelings of emotion?" He said in a way that sounded sort of sarcastic to him. He was a bit confused whose side he was speaking for.

"Did I do wrong?" Animesh asked to measure his act. Trishan shook his head quickly and his tongue-tip came out through his teeth.

"No, no," he cut in on, "it's nothing wrong sending someone a greeting card. I also gave a few cards to my female friends. It's just 'well wishes.'"

Animesh listened to him eagerly, his eyes on Trishan's face in observing manner.

"Look here, friend," he continued, "If you have really loved her, why do you keep away? Why stay in hiding? Face her, and tell her you love her. It's neither sin nor a crime."

Animesh got confused at his emphatic encouragement. He wondered if he was speaking so to advise him or to make fun of it.

"Actually, I didn't have the least bit of a good signal from her as yet, ye know. I suppose she's still thinking whether to move forward or stay back," Animesh explained. "Surely you understand, being a teacher I can't step forward desperately like first-year college kids."

"That's where you are wrong, friend. Love is active equally in every stage of life. To get something you have to risk taking some hindrance. You can't expect to pluck up a rose without being pricked by its thorns."

Animesh kept quiet thinking of his evaluation of love. To see him thoughtfully wordless Trishan said, "Anyway, wait and see then. Good luck!" They parted.

The third day was Saturday, Animesh still had to face the same questions from a few others including girls and he answered them as best as he could according to the closeness of his relationship with them and felt guilty. "God! Protect me from any scandal!" he prayed silently, his eyes closed shortly, his head down. He imagined himself good for nothing: "So timid a person you are! How could you expect a girl's love in life?"

"Feeling sick?" asked Kashinath sitting next to him in the classroom. Professor was not in yet.

"No, I'm alright," he replied and went silent again.

Anxiety must prevail when your proper time is over. Infatuation age was over, in fact. He was above maturity. And it was much like an infatuation. Farmers would get to work in the field while the season is young because they knew late farming would leave them in anxiety. Animesh was in a situation like that. All he wanted was to be successful or get over this situation. He couldn't be swimming in the ocean of anxiety. He wished that she wouldn't make a bedlam about it.

Chapter 17

Animesh did each class in restiveness and he was rather impatient for the latest from Ahalya. After the tensed three days, he saw Anamika in the classroom today. He often stole short gazes at her to read any picture on her face from her reaction but nothing was discovered; she seemed normal in her movements or talking. He thanked God but still he couldn't be cool. After each class, he slipped out of the classroom in the hope of catching Ahalya in a convenient place to get whatever was the news, but no dice.

At last, he caught her walking towards the main gate by the cycle garage as he was coming from the canteen. She had, Mithila and Sangita with her.

"Ahalya?" he called waving his hand at her from a little way off from her left-hand side. She cast a look at him without any expression and walked on.

"Ahalya?" Again he called waving at her. She detected the concerned gaze in his eyes.

"One minute, please." She raised her hand that meant 'wait'. Animesh slowed down to let them move on. A while later, hovering about here and there, upstairs and downstairs, when he was going back to the classroom, Ahalya was coming back from her hostel. She grinned and answered with the same word. "Sorry, I couldn't speak to you at that moment," she apologized.

"I understood," he said, "I didn't mind. You don't know how anxious I have been all the time since that day for the news."

"So you should be," she said admittedly. "It's quite possible."

"What's the news?" he asked anxiously looking down at her face.

"That's why I came over," she replied uncourageously.

Animesh became specially attentive to her words. "The thing is that..." she broke off for a second. "How do I start..." she paused and looked at him helplessly. "You'd better not send her anything again," Ahalya said and looked down at her bag.

"What happened? Has it all been bungled up?" Animesh thought and watched her open her shoulder bag, and take out the envelope and held it out to him. He took it from her hand and looked down at it gloomily. Whenever there is a little adversity, he'd cringe to death and back away but when there is not, he would be dying to get her. It was strange of him.

The news got him like a tornado surrounding his poor heart twisting and crushing it like a helpless tree unable to move out of the whirling tornado.

Ahalya could feel the plight of his mind as she observed him silently. Animesh looked up straight past her as she began again. "Be strong," she said comfortingly. "It does happen in the world of love war, Animesh-da," she continued. "Something obtained through nagging persuasion or tricks would only spill unhappiness, family unrest, arguments, and distress that have enough potency to make a life fragile and put an untimely end."

Admittedly, Animesh was silent as she told him the truth of life. He looked back at her, "What did she say to it when you handed it to her?"

She went back to the scene saying:

"She took it in her hand and looked down at it and turned it over in her hand and stared down at it for a while at the addressee where you'd written her name. By the time other girls came over and stood around her looking down at it eagerly. 'Let us see what,' they demanded. 'Take it out, take it out,' they said persuasively. She took it out and they all leant over it and read the message aloud; Anamika only gazed down at it silently.

"There was almost an invisible chuckle on her closed lips with a touch of shyness. She didn't seem to feel uneasy about the matter and probably she would keep it. Tilli, Sana, and Mithila took it for a funnily interesting matter. When Tilli and Sana emphatically suggested that she should send it back. They also made some ironical humiliating comments; all of it went against you. These two girls turned the situation another way. Anamika became grave right away; the faint chuckle vanished.

'So, many of us have slipped into love affairs, beyond anybody's sight, huh?' Tilli said cuttingly turning her face to Sana, who made a short laugh jointly. This insulting sarcasm gave a blow to Anamika's mind. She got angry at this. 'You can't plant it on me, Tilli,' she said irately, 'It's his idea, not mine. Mind it.' She protested.

'So, he loves you, or else he wouldn't send it to you; he didn't send one to anyone of us, did he?' Sana threw this question more cuttingly. There was a sting in her words, which felt her too bad. Her eyes seemed to have soaked in tears. Anamika's anger diverted over to Animesh who was the main source of this unhappiness.

'Sana, you mean he loved her, but see, there isn't the keyword of 'love' mentioned anywhere here,' Mithila said picking the reasonableness.

'Maybe because he didn't dare use the term 'love' at his first move.' Sana reasoned out."

Animesh felt the palpitation of failure as he heard.

"This time I went into the bathroom," Ahalya said. "When I came back, Anamika said, 'Ahalya, take it and give it back to him. And tell him not to send me anything again.' So, here it is back." Ahalya said in conclusion. She handed the envelope back to him.

"So, she took it out and read it," Animesh pronounced once again to be assured. He had trickily left it unsealed so that she'd be tempted to take it out to see the card or at least, her friends would pursue her to see it out of curiosity. He was right. In a way it meant she accepted the card because after looking at it and reading the message, she would have left it lying somewhere in the room; now she just left it lying somewhere at

Animesh's instead. Only this much was obtained for consolation after the big, tensed mission.

Ahalyla said, "Anyway, don't think over this too much. Studies will be affected." She went toward the classroom. He went back to the canteen and sat with a cup of tea, deeply thoughtful. He was so much broken-hearted that he could neither get on with it nor quit it. It was a more painful situation.

All the same, after analysis what he sensed was that she would have accepted the greetings card unless the spoiler girls had misguided her against him. He broke down at this and thought he wouldn't fall for anybody again and put his mind in studies for better results but it was only for the time being. After two weeks, he felt he couldn't come out of it. He kept asking himself how else he could get to her and win her heart.

Chapter 18

Animesh had been in a nap. A book and a big white copy, half of its page written and an opened pen on it were above his pillow. He had been writing answer notes out of the book lying on his chest with a pillow under. While making notes, he slipped into a siesta. He would always fall asleep while reading or writing something compulsory that deserved serious attention. There was huge pressure of studies with less time in hand, at the same time there was the first ever love for Anamika that kept him distracted. Getting back from the bathroom he got dressed and got out. He had a message in his mobile phone from his Amway Up-line; Kartick, before noon: "See me around 4'clock afternoon, if you can. Important."

Animesh was sitting in Kartick's newly built single room. He looked over at the corridor to the room as Kartick got in.

"Good evening Mr. Thinker," Kartick said jokingly, he often called him 'Thinker' out of the meaning of his family name 'Bhabook' into English.

"Good evening, Mr. Polite." Animesh answered humorously looking up at him smiling. Animesh translated Kartick's surname of 'Bhadra' into 'Polite' for English.

"So you're here," he said.

"Yes, seeing your message," he answered.

Kartick put the towel on the line in the corridor to his room. He sat on his bed.

"What's the summons for?" Animesh asked in amusement.

"Yes, I thought I should have a talk with you." He paused a moment to take a small writing pad. "Up-line called me last night. Saptak hadn't done a single PV in the last four months neither had anyone of his team." He went on. "Because he's in your Down-line, I'd better inform you of it. I found that he neither answered my call nor called me back. I wonder if he was in touch with you."

"I'm guilty, too, the same way as he is; I didn't make a PV in the last three months," Animesh thought to himself.

"No, he wasn't in touch with me. I haven't seen him in the last two months. I was getting convinced that he wasn't suitable for this business, no matter he is a scholar. He couldn't come out of his bad habits even for a week," Animesh said.

"His wife hoped that he would be all right. We reassured her emphatically. But we lost our face to her," Kartick explained. "We had hopes of him, too."

Saptak was a brilliant, smart man to be found one in thousands. He was a PhD in Geology, and a Diploma in Geology from the USA. He quit one company for the other and earned quite good but he blew up his money like waste paper.

"With all immoral impacts in him I shouldn't have brought him in Amway where the least of these things are not allowed," Animesh said regretfully.

"No, there was nothing wrong with getting him into Amway. Or rather you did well to have given him a chance to change himself for his own good. Many people with bad habits have changed. Didn't you hear some of them express their gratitude to Amway for having them brought back to the happy, honest life?" Kartick refuted. "I feel for him to see him ruining miserably before our eyes like that."

"Actually, we can't go against the inevitable of the destined fate," Animesh's evaluation was right.

"Anyway, he's your Direct Leg, it goes over to you to see to it. Tell him to think of the business to some extent," Kartick suggested and reached for his ringing mobile on the book behind him. Animesh watched Kartick receive the call and sensed from his words that it was from an Up-line of Chandan-nagar about another meeting.

Putting down the mobile beside him, he said, "Ayanish Santa, about a meeting."

"Again meeting?" Animesh asked with irritation. "They'll drive me nuts."

Kartick measured his mood silently. Then he said, "Ayanish asked me to go over and get tickets from his house with the right amount of money for the number of tickets we needed."

"Who is coming? What's the ticket price?" Animesh asked.

"A hundred and fifty," Kartick replied.

Animesh nodded, "To hell with the meeting?" he thought to himself. "And where will it be?" he asked aloud.

"At Mahajati Sadan," Kartick replied.

"Calcutta is too far," Animesh said with a touch of avoidance.

"Tell me, how many you think you may need."

"I can't go myself," Animesh answered.

"Hey, don't say 'no'. I feel good to go somewhere without you, I really enjoy with you. Now, without you? No, no, don't say 'no', dear," Kartick said cunningly.

Me too, but I can't go now. The pressure of my studies, you know, has increased a lot and I can't give enough time to it, neither can I give enough time to the business. Until my exams are over I can't afford, honest." He explained but he didn't say the biggest pressure on him was about that girl, Anamika although he wanted to.

Kartick nodded understandably. They both paused for a moment. Now Kartick asked "Then who do you think may go from your team?"

"I don't think anyone will. If I insist, I will have to bear all the expenses for them as I had to so long."

"They have to bear it themselves, why should you? It's against the ethics. Business can't be built this way," Kartick said with emphasis.

"If I tell them to pay me back, they won't say they won't pay back, they'll happily say 'I will pay you', but they don't know themselves if they ever will? You know what Ashu did." Kartick looked eager to listen. "Ashu stopped paying the loan off. I just paid off the rest of his loan in three installments."

Kartick's hand clapped to his head and shook in disapproval.

"That's the reality of the past to realize for tomorrow." Animesh said. "Actually, ye know, Kartick, the business that is fully dependent on people is the hardest to build. It's like the wheels of a vehicle. One of the wheel is disturbed means the whole vehicle is undone."

"Not always," Kartick disapproved, "Many people are coming out successfully in this business. It just depends on the place and environment. Actually, they won't accept training or the ethics. If they get into it today, tomorrow they want the returns to start coming from it. But it's not like that," Kartick refuted with his oracy.

Animesh didn't want it to be longer with any more comment and kept silent till he changed the talk to another way.

"I must go now, getting late," he said.

"Wait a mo!" he waved his hand towards him. "Have tea."

"How far are you, Ma?" Kartick called towards the way in.

"Coming over, son," she answered from her kitchenette. In less than a minute his mother got in with tea and cookies. While having tea together, Kartick told a lot of things about the business.

About half an hour later they were at the outside door, Kartick said, "Anyway, if you stay less active for the few months, it's all right but don't quit."

Animesh turned his head around and looked up at him; his hand gripping at the bicycle handlebar, the bicycle leaning against his body, "I won't," Animesh replied plainly. It didn't sound like coming from the bottom of his heart, "but if the imposed PV is made in the name of products of 'great offers' again and again by Up-lines, it will be harder."

"It won't occur again I suppose. It is very painful."

"Painful it is, indeed, when the guide himself misguides." Animesh thought as he rode his bicycle. But what was worse was that they could never tell any injustice to the still higher Up-Lines.

Chapter 19

In Mid January they fixed a day for a picnic in the open, six kilometers away from Katwa. He took it for a good chance to give a message. The picnic was nice and enjoyable too. The spot was chosen on the bank of an irrigation canal with winter crops all around—potato, lentil fields looked deep green, the flaxseed field looked white, while the mustard fields looked bright yellow waved by the northerly cold wind under the faded blue sky. The mild sun felt warm through the cold wind. The hired cook with his team were cooking on gas, some of the students watched the cooking standing up there, lover couples got themselves away from the crowd to deep chat.

Animesh plucked up more courage and was ready to hand her a hand-written message of his love because just in a few months the session would go to an end. He was looking for a suitable opportunity to hand it over especially beyond the sight of the two villains who might spoil up the whole thing again. Time was ticking away. While looking for a chance, the day grew old. He couldn't make it.

Now the time came for a short function. It was arranged on the green velvet of short grass in a slightly low small piece of land by the cooking spot. A large durrie was laid on the grass and two microphones on the stand. After the short function, it would be the time for lunch and the end of the picnic.

They sang, recited and told comedies as they liked. Anamika sang a song: *For that moon I've quit all, reach it down for me (Oi chader lagi, ami bibagi, dhoriya dao morey chad).*

The significance of her choosing to sing this song made Animesh thoughtful—what did she mean by that? Did she leave hints of proceeding with Animesh's feeling? Did she banter him at his love for her, which meant he was crying for the moon. This vague conundrum left him in another painful anxiety. He jibbed at handing the message over to her and waited for one more suitable situation. He got back home unsatisfied—the college session was running out fast.

Chapter 20

Things had been real crazy for the last two months and none of them had leisure to look the other way; they seemed to be seeing stars, in fact. It was the practice teaching; most important part of the B. Ed courses. The B.Ed. students had to take classes in other schools. It was just over—but still there was no time to relax. From now, the preparation for the final examinations was the greatest headache. Yet there were two more cultural programmes to be performed—one of which was the Debate. All the big kids had some oxygen in the programme with the uprising pressure of work.

The students involved as the secretary of the programme would have to arrange it as per schedule. Animesh and Tilak jointly was the secretary of the Debate. As the secretary, he took a chance to face Anamika for the debate. He went over to her as she was sitting with Sangita, and Shrinika. "Anamika, will you take part in the debate? I think you'll do good in it." He'd asked with uneasiness for he didn't speak to her quite often since the card was sent to her. He wanted to make things easy to pave the way to get ahead.

"Oh no, I won't," she'd answered with her usual smile.

"I heard you wanted to," he said. In fact, he hadn't heard about it. It had been just an excuse to read her mind.

"Whatever you may have heard is wrong. Lots of words are floating in the air like dust particles," she'd answered.

"May be," he said. "Anyway, if you change your mind...," Before he finished, she said quickly, "No, Mr. Bhabook, there's no possibility," she said lightly tossing her hand in jolly way. "You think too much ahead." There was a wicked prick in her tone with a smile.

"That's true. Only I know how much I think and who I think of, but how can I ever have you realize it," he thought.

He got back to his place. Her simple general talk gave him a measure that she didn't want to avoid him. And he was optimistic.

It was the debate day today. Professor Arun K. Roy and Prof. R. H. Dutta headed the Debate programme. Mr. Roy, who was a professor of Economics of this college, was the external expert to preside over the programme. Animesh felt good to see him after sixteen years. He went back to the session during the time when he did the Higher Secondary courses here. Prof. Roy used to take Economics classes back then. His sweet, smart voice had touched him very much. In so many years the professor didn't change much in his physical appearance except his hair that had been thin on the scalp then went bald now and all the hair turned almost white. He had a wide black moustache that turned all white and narrower but he still held the stout structure.

The debating, however, didn't come much alive. After the Debate was over, Professor Roy discussed about the performance: "Before I announce the results of today's debate, I need to talk it over." He looked at Prof. Dutta and spoke something which was not heard. Then he started: "The subject of today's debate was: *The School Teachers Must not Do Private Tuitions*. It was a very contemporary subject and widely-talked matter with discontent. Teachers signed the bond of not doing private tuitions by order of the despotic communist government," he paused. "Those who spoke against spoke well enough, but those who spoke in favour spoke well anyway, though I had expected it to be still better because there was a very strong point against the government's slanted order that could have been added," he continued. "The question is: Can the government decide on teachers' tuition beyond the specified hours of the service to the government? Can the government impose its harmful whim on its employees? What the government can do is to make sure that its employees do the desirable service to it and if necessary to make sure that they are not involved in any criminal activities or anti-national activities after their duty hours are over." He took another pause.

Animesh looked bright here, he smiled and remembered he had often spoken the same point in his school staffroom that it was all injustice done by the government. He had emphatically opined that the teachers' union should have sued the Government against the order. He thought that they got a job to work for the government because the government wanted them at its service based on their own educational qualifications. But it didn't mean that the government could order them anything, or had the right to torture them. Unfortunately, Animesh couldn't take part in the debate because he was one of the organizers of the Debate of the cultural programme.

Professor went on. "But none of the debaters touched this great point. The other points you picked up were acceptable somehow," he paused again, and took a sip of water from the glass on the table.

"Anyway, here we come to announce the results of the debate," he said and picked up the result sheet in his hand. "The first position goes to Trishan Mouli, the second to Arnab, and the third to Mithila Bayen. All of you are requested to come onto the dais."

The winners were given their certificates through claps, and smiles. Professors gave each of them a handshake.

Chapter 21

Time really ticked away fast, say, too damn fast. It was high summer in West Bengal; May was in its first week. Summer fruits had already infested the market. And this year was a mango year. Every alternative year is a mango year because mango trees can't recover its damage from fruition and grow mangoes every year. So, they take a break.

Animesh was eating mango in a bowl that was given by his mother. In the late afternoon, especially after lunch fruits were nice to enjoy and good for health but it wouldn't be possible for the ordinary people to buy enough fruits unless they have them grown on their home trees. Almost all families in the village hereabouts had mango-jackfruit-guava trees at home.

While eating the sliced juicy mango sitting in his room of the new L-pattern house whose outside plastering was yet to be done, Animesh looked around at the cream coloured walls whose smell of the paint was obviously felt in the nose, the single-panelled wooden door painted brown, and the new fan on the snow-white ceiling. He felt happy and satisfied.

"Who could ever think we the small fry of the one-time poor people would ever have a good ideal home like this with a mobile phone, a colour TV and a government job in it?" he thought to himself. There was a time when all the folks of the family would tremble in fear of the smashing Kalbaishakhi storms. Many a time, seeing the storm-clouds sparking and rumbling in the western sky, his father would have to rush back home closing his kiosk hurriedly in the evening to be with them because they would be scared stiff of the crazy storms. None of the family would have to be scared of it any more. From now on, he wouldn't have to worry every year in the rains for fear of devastating floods and look for a shelter at somebody else's. He knew how hardship and trouble they had to go through during the last two great floods.

Now his heavenly father came into his thought. He felt extremely sorry for his late father. He couldn't see all these successes of his sons. He'd had a dream of a brick-built house. He'd believed that his eldest son would get a government job. Animesh had that job today but he was no more. The cruel disease and fortune snatched him away from the family in 1997 suffering from the worst hardship of breath trouble. The man had to go through all hardship all through his life since he had come empty-handed into India leaving behind his ancestor's homestead in the then East Pakistan at his youth and find a place to live sheltered and eke out a meagre living out of the little money he used to make.

Animesh heard his mother tell about the hardship of those days when they had to go through only one humble meal a day during a famine-like situation. Animesh was merely a small kid then. After those horrible days were over, days changed for the better and better to what it is today with ups and downs in between. While thinking, Animesh's eyes got fogged up and then the sight blurred from the welled up tears in his eyes.

"O God!" He prayed with regret, "What justice was that on my father?" He asked the heaven under his breath. "You gave him all miseries all through his life. But you didn't give him the minimum peace and happiness at his last years! We couldn't give him the right treatment only because of lack of money. We couldn't even give him the cool air from an electric fan that he needed most when he suffered from the breathlessness." The electric line was not installed in his turf yet. Drops of tears rolled silently down his cheeks. The bowl of mango was still held in his hand, his unseeing eyes at the wall, the face saddened. He didn't feel like eating the mango anymore. The mango that he was eating also grew on the tree that his father had planted. He slowly put down the bowl on the red-coloured floor.

It was then Maheshpati Munsi came to see him. He stood at the stairs to the veranda. "Are you in, son?" he called. Animesh knew his voice. He adored him a lot. He was years older than his father and they two were friends. Animesh wiping his eyes on his handkerchief stepped out of the door and said, "Yes, uncle, come in." It was the man who had sheltered Sudhindra with his family in his second mud house opposite his first one for over a month until Sudhindra had his own hut made up after he'd left his homestead at the neighbouring village of Berah twenty-five years back and came over here to Inrani Pargana.

"Sit down uncle," Animesh said to him gesturing at the chair he had been sitting and brought another from the balcony for himself to sit face to face. The scrawny tall guy sat down looking around the room.

"So, you've had a nice house now. Then why get late for the 'home laxmi' now? Mahespati suggested. 'Home laxmi' meant an ideal good mannered wife taking care of the family, compared with 'Goddess Laxmi' who is believed to give wealth to people and care for them. This man had informed him about a bride soon after he'd had the job but he'd said then, "I haven't got a house yet. How can I ask people in? Where should I seat them?" Now he had nothing to say. He felt uneasy at Munsi's suggestion. How could he tell about his weakness for Anamika to him? He hesitantly answered, "Yes, I'll do it."

"Then, let's go with me this Sunday. I'll take you somewhere. There is a good bride; graduate, cool, homely, looking nice. Her father's a retired school teacher. They will spend a lot on their daughter's marriage," he stopped and waited for his answer looking at his face.

"Where's it?" Animesh asked weakly.

"It's near Katwa," Munsi answered enthusiastically.

"It's too near," he said, "I don't want to make relations so near at a place."

"How's it so near?" He asked surprised, "It's Katwa. So many people have married there. People even marry on their own turf. I'm not talking of someone on the turf."

"That's true, mostly from love affairs. But I haven't got through with my B. Ed course yet. Now I'm too busy to make time."

"Can't you make just two hours in the afternoon?" He asked earnestly.

"This time it's in no way possible." Animesh's tone was emphatic. "I can't make time even to die. See the plight," He gestured at the bed where books and copies were open in a clutter.

His red tongue flicked quickly out of his beetle-eaten mouth between the rows of teeth cutting on it and he shook his head. "Don't speak ominous like this," he said. "I understand." With a short pause he asked," How long is it still to go?"

"Three months," Animesh answered.

"Okay, let it go over, and tell me." Munsi said sort of broken hearted.

So, saying Maheshpati got up and left. Animesh thought he escaped it somehow. He couldn't think of any woman other than Anamika whose face floated before his eyes every so often. How could he ever think of any other woman!

Chapter 22

It was the annual function day, the last and biggest cultural programme of the session, Animesh came to college a little later than usual. All the same there weren't many kids yet except the cultural secretary, four boys from the decorator's to set up the sound system and decorating the function hall. Finding nothing to do, he went down the stairs with lazy steps and stopped at the main gate looking farther up at the street. Girls of the morning section and some other boys were milling around. He found none of his pals around. So, he turned and went into the canteen and spent some time at his usual place thinking many things, as well as reciting the poem in the back of his mind. He found he still got stuck or the intonation wouldn't come right somewhere in the poem. He watched girls, and boys talking and laughing sitting in the middle of the canteen. A while later he found Utpal Sau walk in lazily before he ordered for tea.

Animesh waved him over as soon as their eyes met. Utpal came over, "Animesh-da, how long here?" he asked and sat face to face. "Some time ago, brother," Animesh replied, "Better you came, I felt too bored and stupid all by myself with the junior kids here."

Animesh went to the service window, ordered for tea and cookies for themselves, and came back to his seat. Utpal was a fair-skinned, good-looking polite kid, a lot younger than Animesh. He would mostly wear light coloured shirts. It was him that tided them over with the tabla in all the programmes. He was going to take part in the pantomime today.

The tea man called and Utpal got them. While eating cookies and sipping at the tea, the conversation went on.

"How are you prepared for the pantomime?" Animesh asked.

"It's alright. There is no talking in it, only mute acting. And besides I did it before in my home town." Utpal replied. Animesh nodded with his description.

"That's why I requested you take a part, but..."

"Oh, I've got the stage fright, brother. I never did programmes on the stage except for two small poem recitations and that too, to my students in my school programmes." Animesh took another sip from his cup.

"Then, aren't you going to do anything today?" He asked.

"Yes, I'm gonna recite a poem, a small one, however, English," Animesh said, "But still I find it jumpy and I'm stumbling at reciting it in mind. I wonder if it will come out right."

"Don't think of it too much. It'll be nice in your way of recitation."

They kept silent for a while with the empty earthen cups in front of them.

Suddenly Utpal changed the matter. "It's gonna end up; only a little more than a month to go and then the exams, and then it's all over; everybody'll be back to their nests like birds in the evening," Utpal said happily. He had reason to be happy. He wasn't a deputed student like Animesh who got paid as well as enjoying the studentship. He had no tension. But Utpal had to carry all expenses from his father's pocket.

"Yes, Utpal, it seems time's flying by. A wonderful year, man, with many kids from different places spent like one family,..."

Animesh stopped hopelessly. And '*she*' floated up in his mind's eye. It was then Utpal hit the right thing. "Did you see 'your her'?"

"My her!" Animesh smiled wryly shaking his head in a pretending surprise. In fact, he didn't dare think her to be his. He couldn't impress her.

"Don't prick into my heart by saying 'she's mine'. I'm no good at being romantic. This 'love business' is not for everybody, ye know, unless you're a fraud, a loafer, a liar, pretending yourself somebody in hell when you're not, and so on, running after them obstinately..."

Animesh paused seeing Utpal looking over at the door distracted by something. "Above all, you need stars," Animesh said touching his forehead with the tip of his forefingers.

"I've got nothing to say to it. That's about astrology. But I saw her today and thought of her differently."

"Differently! —means?" Animesh was more anxious than he was curious. The bad idea came to his mind. He thought somebody else occupied her heart. "What did you see? Tell me," He demanded.

"She adorned herself very well today, gorgeously and she looked so wonderful in a saree like a beauty queen from Tolleywood." Girls in a sari always look more beautiful and taller than in any other dresses.

"You'd said one day that she looked like a trout fish," Animesh thought to himself but he didn't let it out on his face but slightly chuckled.

"It's good of you, you discovered her at last," Animesh said. "Anyway, where did you see her?"

"There at the hostel gate, she was going towards the shops with her hostel friends."

"Who were with her?" Animesh asked impatiently.

"Ahalya, Debosmita, Mithila, and your enemies," he replied. He meant Tilli and Sana.

"Oh, enemies," Animesh intoned, "Those enemies in all the places, in all the countries, all over the world through ages since people learnt to live in groups have spoiled things up. The overwhelming fate has made them lucky only to break, not to make, to pull you down, not to help you up, to kill, not to save." He went on.

"That's one of the biggest troubles for a society. If you take it for a nation, there breaks out wars for which only little people have to pay for their conspiracies, for their play-around.

That's it," Animesh explained.

Utpal nodded in agreement. "That's why I keep away from any trouble." Utpal said.

They kept silent for a moment while Animesh thought of what Utpal said and became restive to have an absorbing look at her.

"Let's get up, see how far it is to the programme," Animesh suggested and stood up.

Chapter 23

They sat in a group in a middle bench on the left side row furthest from the door, it was their usual place. Arnab sat ahead of them with his closer friends. The professors sat on the front benches of the middle row. The stage was well decorated.

Animesh's eyes occasionally went over to Anamika as usual. She sat in the middle of a middle bench of the middle row, farther behind the professors.

Utpal was right. Animesh was spellbound to her beauty today. She wore a sari in other programmes, too, but this time she looked better than ever. It seemed to him that the whole world's beauty was poured on her, in her light orange-pinkish sari with the same colored blouse, golden oval patterned earrings and light-orange lipstick, well treated face and nicely done shiny-black wavy hair with a string of white mogra flowers around and the sloe eyes of hers, and uneven teeth with one tooth impacted added extra beauty, which seemed incomparable. The more he saw her, the more he was enchanted when she spoke to her friends with smiles on her pink lips. The jollity seeped out of her heart and showed on her face. It seemed to him he was forgetting his poem.

The programme went on through whisper-chatting between pals sporadically in the hall. Animesh's being a participant in the programme was bothered with himself; he was once pulled by her attraction and again by his recitation of the poem and again by the ongoing programme on the stage. So, he was half attentive. Sometimes, he took part with his friends in commenting on the performances, but quite often his eyes stubbornly went over to her to feast his eyes on her beauty to his heart's content, and above all his palpitation hammered him under his chest with increased cold waves sweeping through his heart whenever he suddenly remembered his turn on the stage. So, he tried to recite the poem in mind to bring it out with the proper rhythm and intonation.

Anamika Sen , Debsmita Saha, Ahalya Adhikary, Sarbani Pal and other girls sang, of the boys sang Kashinath, Shibansu, Jaynal, and Nirnoy. Recitations, comedies, songs, and dances went in between. Arnab's comedy made the audience roll over with laughter. The programme became lively in the middle. Professors were enchanted with performances of their students.

Animesh had bought a Nikkon camera a few months before the Rajgir Excursion Tour. It was left on Tilak's hand to take photos from the beginning. He was doing his duty all right.

It was Animesh's turn now. Akash Biswas, who hosted all through the programme announced: "Now another recitation of a different taste," he paused and lifted his eyes from the programme list on the clip board in his hand and looked over at the audience, "An English poem—by Animesh Bhabook." Akash looked over at Animesh, who stood up from his seat to hit the stage. He felt another cold wave of tension surging across his heart and this time down to the stomach. He took a deep breath and let it out before he got out of the benches. The heart was racing now seemed to be making him feel choked with saliva in his throat.

He climbed on to the dais with an artificial smartness, and stood behind the microphone and noticed Tilak attempting the camera to snap his photos.

To feel easy and mitigate his tension, he took another deep breath and first he began to speak something in introduction: "Good afternoon to you all in the audience. I'm not used to be on the stage, and naturally, it does a thing to my heart, to speak frankly." He paused shortly and gulped down stealthily. Wasting this little time on the introduction helped him be easy enough. Then he said again, "I'm going to recite an English poem, and—here it goes—'Geetanjali 92', composed by, the World Poet Rabindranath Tagore." With a short pause he began:

> I know that the day will come
> When my sight of this earth shall be lost,
> And life will take its leave in silence,
> Drawing the last curtain over my eyes.
> Yet stars will watch at night,
> And morning rise as before
> And hours heave like sea waves
> Casting up pleasures and pains.
> When I think of this end of my moments,
> The barrier of the moments breaks,
> And I see by the light of death
> Thy world with its careless treasures.
> Rare is its lowliest seat, rare is its meanest of lives.
> Things that I longed for in vain,
> And things that I got—let them pass.
> Let me but truly possess the things
> That I ever spurned and overlooked.

He thanked the audience and got off the stage. There was a light clapping from the audience. Right away his palpitation and worries began to seep out of him fast. He walked back to his place without looking at the audience. He saw Anamika sitting on the edge of the bench that had been the third bench behind his own. It was not known when and why she was there. On meeting her eyes, he noticed she made as if she wanted to say something. But alas! Here too, he made a blunder; probably the biggest blunder ever, might be from the tension of his reciting. He turned his face to his seat and sat down without giving attention to her trend.

This strange behaviour of him cut into her heart subtly but seriously, which was evident when her face suddenly turned grave. Maybe she liked his recitation in American accent and intonation.

Maybe she wanted to felicitate him. But he himself bungled it up once again.

The friends near him praised his performance but it didn't feel that much to him. He thanked them morally, but his mind went back too often to the scene behind him driving him into another emotional upset. He closed his eyes and tried to envisage the picture of her face of that very moment—"Did she want to tell me something about my recitation? Did I do another blunder by turning my face away from her? Why in hell would I ever turn away from her at that crucial moment?" He asked himself. He turned around his head and looked back at her. On meeting with her eyes and a little easiness in her, he would catch it and speak to her to take the sting out. But she looked grim, occupied by her own world and wasn't the least bit eager to say a word to his belated eagerness, neither did she let her eyes meet his, either. He did it twice. But no dice!

Feeling uneasy, she went back to her middle place to her friends. Here he felt even sadder and guiltier. He sat like a stone shaking his head lightly in curse from time to time beyond anyone's notice as he thought of the scene over and over again. He felt that his eyes seemed to thrust tears out for his unmanageable blunder but he had to control it because he was in public. His mouth narrowed, his face turned black like nimbus clouds in the rains. How many more blunders? There was no knowing. He asked himself over and over again—would he ever have another chance to make up for the blunder? But there wasn't much time for him; the college session neared its end.

Chapter 24

In the next few weeks nothing positive happened although he tried to create a situation that could delete the feeling of that function-day. She seemed no way to get ahead nor to say 'no' to him directly. On the contrary Animesh couldn't come back either.

Near the end of the next week, he came across Ahalya at the door of the library hall as she was getting out through the door and went a few steps past him throwing a smile of formality but stopped short calling behind, "Animesh-Da? Just a minute."

Animesh, too stopped short at the door at her call before she stepped back to him. He moved over to the parapet to let people pass from the door or along the narrow veranda, Ahalya in front of him.

"I hear it was your camera that the pictures of the function were taken in?" She said in a rising tone.

"Yes, it was mine," he replied pleasantly, "The one, if you mean, was in Tilak's hand."

"Yes, I'm talking about that one," she said quickly with a big smile. Animesh got her right away what she wanted to say but he pretended innocent.

"So?" He asked smiling back at her.

"Give us the photos of us, will you?" She requested.

"Certainly," Animesh replied, "You must get them."

"Please, give us, and hers too" she urged, "as soon as you can, please."

"Hers!?" He frowned staring down at her pretentiously just to hear more about her.

"Your 'she', I mean—Anamika." She tried to make it clear. "You stubborn silly! As if butter wouldn't melt in your mouth," she said casting a funny look at him. It was a sort of appeasement.

"You still say she's mine!?" He asked surprised and tut-tutted and shook his head.

87

"Animesh-da, I understand how you feel inwardly, what feels you like in the deep of your heart, no matter what you say outwardly. Not only me, everybody knows it."

Now Animesh lowered his voice and said grimly, "If I could have said she was mine, who'd have been happier than me in the world?" he asked regretfully.

"That's your failure, Animesh-da. Your stupidity. You can get nothing unless you make a move," Ahalya accused him plainly.

Animesh swore his failure in his mind. "That's why he couldn't stay in peace." All the same he thought differently. "Ahalya, loving and being loved is not for everybody on the earth and especially not for me, according to what it figures till now. I'm a dope about it; a great stupid who doesn't know the ways of love—the 'love attitude', love language, coaxing, … and who even can't catch an opportunity either. You're right, certainly. It's my failure."

Forcing a deep sigh of hopelessness he said, "I stupidly did a few blunders and mistakes and bungled my opportunities."

She said, "That's why I say, you too, could have had it if you had been a little bold and active," she said. "It doesn't come off a one-sided move. You too have to step forward. If one takes three steps forward, the other can take one step. We girls can't be as easy and cheap as you lads can, especially in our country."

"I did the much I was able to, sis, but …

She broke in, "If you do things the wrong way and if the results don't come your way, who will you blame?" With a short pause she said, "Some icebergs are too big and too hard in cold climates. But they too must melt in the right warmth. That's what you'd have to know and go ahead accordingly. In fact, you lose your faith with a little adversity. You aren't supposed to be so. Be confident enough and bold a little where necessary. Girls often try a man's confidence and smartness. If you can pass the trial, you're the winner."

"I swear your complaints about me. I am timid, un-smart, I lack confidence," he said admitting her nice explanation. For a moment the scene of that very day flashed back before his eyes how he had turned his face away from her after he had recited the poem. He looked down thoughtfully at the floor. By the little time, how many people brushed past them, they didn't know. He got back to the present.

"Anyway," he said raising his head up at her face. "Does she really want the photos of her?" He asked intending to dig into Anamika's eagerness for the photos.

"Yes, she does want them."

"Okay, I'll ask her," Animesh said casually but he took it serious wanting to fade the bad feeling away from his behavior of that day. He got some oxygen from the talk.

"Yeah, go 'n ask 'er. But don't be late about the photos." So saying she started on her way.

"Give 'em next week," she called and disappeared at the bend of the veranda.

Animesh walked into the library study room, in front of him and behind the grilled partition was the service counters of the big library. He chuckled to himself contentedly. He knew their photographs would be in demand. He had expected them to ask for their photos. It could be the last chance for him to correct the blunders and go ahead afresh for her.

He took the English questions from the counter and left the library room.

In the first week of June, Animesh happened to see Anamika luckily in a convenient place when she was coming up from the canteen with Ahalya, Debsmita and Tilli. His heart started throbbing as he thought of asking her of the photos. He took a deep breath and plucked up courage as they came up. From a little distance he gazed at her; her eyes were down at the ground as she approached, not wanting to look at him.

"Anamika," Animesh called loud enough, looking straight up at her face, sort of desperately. She looked up at him. "Just a moment." He raised his hand for a signal to stop. She stopped right off and so did her companions.

"Do you want the photos of you of the function?" He asked plainly.

"Yes, I do want them," she said with a smile as usual; that 'winning smile'.

It was a long time since he saw her seraphic smile from close quarters. It filled his heart.

"Okay, I'll give yours and Ahalya's together," he said happily. Ahalya chuckled wickedly beside her.

"How many copies do you want?" He asked her.

"How many..." she said thoughtfully, "one copy each."

Again thinking a little she said, "No, no, two copies."

Then again she hesitated and thought, then said, "How many can there be altogether?"

"More or less eight photos, I suppose, I mean the specially selected ones," he replied thoughtfully.

"Then one copy of each, ...yes, one copy each," she concluded finally. "But when, when can we have them?" This time she spoke with jollity and her natural dramatic attitude. There was no sign that reflected she was hurt or offended."

"By next week," Animesh said at a guess.

"How come?" She expressed doubt. "Study leave is beginning in five days."

"Oh! So it is!" Animesh exclaimed thoughtfully, his hand went under his chin.

"Okay, you'll get them before we leave college. Don't worry. Actions speak louder than words. You'll see."

They parted off for the opposite ways. Animesh walked towards the canteen. Pleasure was back on his face. He thought that things were changing but it was too late when the session came close to an end. He regretfully thought, "If only I had some more time in hand…?

Chapter 25

Animesh did want to handover the photos before the study leave started and make a way to make things easy with her but it was no way possible. So, the study leave started and ended. And then the exams began and were going to an end.

The examination center was about four kilometers away from Katwa College. The exam hall on the first floor of the Bengal Institute of Technology was a large one, full of examinees. A little whisper made it rather noisy in the hall. Each bench had two examinees.

Today most of them didn't seem to take it that serious because it was the last day of examinations of the B. Ed session on the additional subject. Examinees talked a little more than the previous days, which made the invigilators sort of worried and angry. They warned them from time to time, commanding irately, "Don't talk. You should remember you're teachers." That was true. They were made teachers with the year-long training. So, they felt sort of embarrassed to act otherwise. But still they couldn't help asking their friends where they got stuck. In fact, if one or two marks managed this way, who would let them away? Besides, the old brain didn't hold things in its memory as it had at their youth.

"Don't talk. I'm telling you several times. Don't talk. Be fair with the examination." This time, suddenly, Arnab fell in target of a young man invigilator who was one of the three in the hall. He was stricter than others. He watched over him and warned him a few times. Arnab went quiet, but after a moment, he asked Mithila another question. She told him the answer.

"Hello, you, don't you know when you're spoken to?" the invigilator warned him again snapping his fingers at him angrily. Arnab got quiet again and chuckled. After a little while, he called in a loud whisper, "Akash, Group C, 6.3."

Akash slightly twisted his body and gestured at his exam paper, "I ain't done it."

At this the invigilator's got sore. He stomped over to Arnab, "If you speak again, I'll remove you from here," he snapped pointing his finger straight at him.

"Ok, then it'll be better for me, sir. She can't answer my questions, see," Arnab said with a short laugh. There went a ripple of soft laughter across the front of the hall from those who watched the drama.

Arnab's reply was cuttingly funny that made him even more sore but he was speechless. The invigilator was of about the same age as Arnab. He couldn't protest nor could he remove him from there. Feeling defeated and embarrassed, he let out an angry, grave sound, "Hmmhh?!" and moved over to the other side casting a firing look at his face. It was the last comedy from Arnab that his friends had ever had.

Animesh checked the time. A little more than half an hour left. He turned the question paper over and found there were two more big questions still to answer.

The Work Education questions were easy and common. His pen ran like crazy. He had planned to hand in his exam paper at least 15 minutes earlier and wait for Anamika at the gate. He had his promise to keep that he would give her the photographs before she left college. Meeting Anamika was most important because she'd leave for home. At the same time, the exam was most important, too; it was the final exam for an academic degree. He checked the time from time to time and wrote on. Being torn between the two most important situations made him inattentive and nervous that made him make more wrongs in writing faster and fall behind for crossing out the wrongs and rewriting them. It was a horrible situation he'd ever been in. Sometimes he overlooked small mistakes and kept on rushing with the writing—no wasting of time. He somehow managed to finish it only minutes before the final bell rang.

When Animesh hurried out to the precinct, he saw Anamika walking out talking with her friend Mithila, Ahalya, Sangita and Tilli. And this time, unfortunately, Kashinath and Utpal shouted to him from the back. "Animesh, wait, Animesh, wait." They called repeatedly. Animesh was at a distance on the institute ground. "That's fucked it. Shit!" he pronounced instinctively. He turned around and called them over. "Come hotfoot." He had to stop unwillingly. He clucked his tongue from impatient and annoyance; "Oh, God! Just two minutes earlier if I had come out!" he murmured with deep regret. He waved at Kashinath and Utpal to hurry up, but they seemed too careless to care his urge. They weren't to be blamed for that; they didn't have the torment in their heart, neither did they know what Animesh was so anxious for.

He looked at Anamika and back at Kashinath—the distance from Anamika grew longer and longer. The attraction to her pulled him to take a few steps forward but Kashinath's call pulled him to stop; he looked back at Kashinath and stopped short for them to catch up with him. Such an odd situation he was in that he neither could wait for them nor could he rush after Anamika leaving them behind, saying, "To hell with you guys. Take your time and come comfortably." He started walking hesitantly again a little fast, again slowly looking back at Kashinath and Utpal waving at them to come faster, again back at Anamika. It kept going this way with distance growing as well his worries.

At last when this troika came past the main gate, they fell a lot behind Anamika's group. Animesh watched her cross the main road eagerly and got on the grassy narrow gauge railway lines whose stones mostly subsided in the soil, and green grass covered the surface. The bus road and the railroad ran side by side for about a kilometer. With deep sadness, Animesh watched that they were walking with pleasure making fun with each other, hand in hand, and laughing and enjoying moving over the narrow gauge track, the open lowland marshes and the farming land on their right hand side. Kashinath and Utpal asked him about the questions of the exam. Animesh gave slapdash answers to their questions with his restive mind while walking down the macadam road, his eyes and attention all went over to Anamika's movement. The girls got off the railway line and got on the macadam road near the bus stop at the T-junction where the railway track distanced from the macadam road. He wished she wouldn't get the bus until he arrived there but bad luck again, a bus did come from the Bolpur-Katwa route and stopped. Hopelessly he watched them get on the bus from the distance. "I knew I couldn't catch them up. Shit!" He thought sadly and wished that their bus would come right away.

They were at Katwa bus terminus ten minutes late. Kashinath and Utpal shook hands with him in courtesy. "We were friends for a year and we're parting now. Maybe we'll see each other again sometime somewhere, or may be not—God on high knows." Animesh's hands were in their hands standing face to face but his thought ran riot in his head how quickly he could leave and go over to her. Maybe, her bags were all packed up, and she would leave for home right away.

"Anyway, stay lucky and nice wherever you are," Animesh said. "Forgive if I went wrong or hurt you," Kashinath said. Utpal said, "Don't keep these in mind."

They split. Animesh didn't look any other way then. He rushed for the hostel to keep his promise, to grab a last look at her before she quit Katwa.

Chapter 26

Animesh took a short look at Matangini Ladies' Hostel close to the boundary wall on his left, then at the college building ahead of him for the last time. There was none from the hostel around to send a message to Anamika. He waited for a while thinking, then leaving the bicycle on its stand at the side of the hostel entrance, he opened the small grill gate, went in and walked across the walled space to the grill door which was at one end of the veranda. He took out the two envelopes from his bag and pushed the bell-button twice. It didn't ring. Before he knocked on the grill, a girl came out with a bag in her hand and opened the grill door. He knew her by face in class. "Is Anamika in?" he asked.

"Yes," She replied quickly and called "Anamika? Somebody is here to see you." She walked out.

When he got ahead a little down the veranda near to their door, Anamika came out and got scared to see him walking up straight. "Oh, no, no, no, no, don' come in, don' come in," she said frighteningly shaking her head and hand before him. Puzzled Animesh quickly said, "oh, okay, okay." And he came out of the grill-door as quickly. "Sorry, sorry," he said guiltily and embarrassedly. It was ignorance of him that he didn't know that men were not allowed in. Coming out of the grill-door, he stood at the steps. "Oh hell! Again I have done a big mistake," he thought sadly. It began to prick into his mind sharply. His face shrunk. "Blunders in a row, one after the other—oh God! What am I good at?" He thought regretfully.

Anamika came out of the grill too and stood on the cemented walk. Ahalya, too, came out and stood beside her. He held out the two envelopes to Anamika under Ahalya'a eager eyes. "The photos that I'd promised you." He smiled, but in that smile, there wasn't any touch of naturalness or simplicity, There was a tremendous feeling of crime and embarrassment, and disgust for himself for his misdoings.

"Thank you," they both said smilingly. "How much for these?" Anamika asked.

"No, no, you don't have to pay. It's just a gift from me," Animesh said quickly in polite refusal.

"No, no, you must take their cost." Anamika insisted. "Or else I can't take it."

Animesh fell into a problem here. If he could have given them as a gift, it could have taken the sting out of the embarrassing situation a bit. Ahalya couldn't decide which way to support; for gifts or for paying for the photos that he intently intended to gift them.

"I'll be right back." On saying this Anamika went in, certainly to get money.

"So, she shall pay for the photos!" Animesh said gloomily. "Why pay for them? I want to give you these for gifts," he said to Ahalya.

Ahalya smiled in answer. She was willing to take them for gift. But she couldn't now. "No, no, take the price for them," she said weakly. "Let me pay you for mine," She said wanting to get in. He stopped her, "Wait, wait. Why can't you take them as a gift?" He asked.

"It's not the things that I can't take them as a gift, but..." Ahalya said when Anamika came back and held out a fifty-rupee note to him. "Here you are—for both of us."

"Not so much." Animesh protested.

"Okay, keep it all." She insisted.

"No, it doesn't go," he said and paid her the balance back.

He didn't feel like moving out right away from them and he didn't have any excuses either to spend a little more with them. He stood there kind of nervously and sadly being pricked by the mistake and looked down at the ground and again at them to gain some time. Nobody had anything to say anymore. Then he spoke out, looking at Anamika. "So, you're leaving for home today?"

"No, tomorrow morning," she replied.

"One thing," he said but hesitated. They both looked at his face for him to say 'the one thing'. "Will you give me your phone number, please?" He asked. There are three more photos of you. I can give you later. In fact, there wasn't any.

Anamika replied, "I don't have a number." Animesh noticed her graveness on her face now. He was sort of surprised and he couldn't quite believe her answer.

"Oh, I see," he said hopelessly slightly bending his head down and looked the other way, and stood speechless for a moment again. She couldn't miss another picture of dismay over his face. "Okay then," he said, and took a piece of paper out of his shirt pocket and held it out to her. "Keep it with you, please, and give a call. Any time." She took a brief look at the slip where his mobile number and his name was written. She held it with the photo envelopes in her hand.

"Okay, take care, you both. Stay lucky. Call me, please; I have something to say to you." He said and took a last intent, heartfelt look at the sweet loving face and turned around and walked out of the compound slowly.

Out at the entrance of the hostel compound, he turned his bicycle and looked back once again thoughtfully with a magnetic gaze at the hostel. They had already gone in. He couldn't tear himself away from the place; but he had to. He climbed the bicycle lazily with his leg swung from the ground and rode on slowly, his head down from the sting of the last blunder and worries.

He was extremely sad to think that he would be away from college for keeps. He had this appreciable student life after one and a half decades but it was only for one session, which was in fact no more than six months; The rest of the months went for vacation, practice teaching in local schools, preparatory leave for exams, and results. What was left for studentship pleasure, for chatting, for loafing around, or ....? The more he thought the more it hurt him deep in his heart. "Won't I be able to see her ever again?" He wondered. He only knew he would be living in the heart of Burdwan town but she in Kanchannagar—not too far away from the town.

Chapter 27

Makhom opened the doors of the room and turned on the light and fan. He was the assistant caretaker of New Burdwan Hotel, younger than Animesh. He got in. He saw the left side seat of the two in it was empty. It was for him. When Makhom dusted off the plank-bedstead, he put his suitcase and bags on the next bedstead. Animesh sat down on it.

"Okay, then rest now," Makhom said. He handed over the key to him. "If you need me, call me over." He left.

Animesh looked around the small room. The other plank-bedstead had the bedding rolled up in a flat shape. There were pictures of God and Goddess on the shelves of the door-less wall-cupboard, worshipped with garland and flowers that still looked fresh enough. "The guy is pious enough," he thought to himself. He laid out the bedding on the old bedstead; a durrie and three bed sheets, a mosquito net and a pillow—that was all. When he'd had a quick wash in the bathroom, the sun was yet to set. He sat on the bed to relax. He was feeling uneasy a bit. He didn't feel it right to live in a shared room with somebody else. He regretted for his old single-bedded room at the farthest end on this ground floor. He lived there privately listening to English, Bengali or Hindi songs, and the BBC or VOA programmes without disturbing anybody or being disturbed. That room went to Antu after he'd left it for his B. Ed studies.

An hour later it was evening. Animesh was reading a book when a tall, fair-skinned, smart, medium healthy stern-looking man came in and looked down at him curiously. He had sober clothes on; an off-white shirt tucked in his grey trousers and black shoes on his legs.

"I have been put in here," Animesh said plainly.

"Yes, I was told of you," he answered with a thin smile. He put down his briefcase on a box at the foot of the bed and sat down to take off his shoes. Then he wore a towel around his waist, took off his garments and he went out to the bathroom. Animesh saw many boxes of medicines under the bedstead. He seemed to be a high profile person to Animesh that caused uneasiness in him. He began to think of moving out to a rented room in another turf for he never lived in a mess or hostel in a shared room.

Back from the bathroom, the man unrolled the bed, straightened it and sat gratefully. He called Makhom over. He appeared at the door. The man said, "Two teas and two bread toasts, baked-brown." Animesh watched him gesturing at him and give Makhom a ten rupee-note. But Animesh politely refused to eat on him, but the man insisted.

While eating they talked about their field of work, their names, and the place they were from. The man introduced himself as Arijit Maity from Calcutta. He was a medical field officer on sales. He was nosy enough. Animesh's days started going with that man.

Chapter 28

He was going back home at the weekend. He sat by a right side window seat of the Raja bus. He looked out at the narrow gauge railway track by the BIT College. It gusted a cold thrust into his heart. "That's the place!" he thought and reminisced the scene of Anamika's walking down the track with her friends, and how he crazily tried catch up with her. That sweet moment would never come back again. He sighed gloomily. Every time he went back home on holidays he would look at this place sadly.

In Burdwan Animesh's hungry eyes had always been on the lookout for Anamika hoping to see her by chance on her way somewhere, or so. Many times over he went out riding his bicycle and roamed about the streets or at the station square and farther towards Kanchan-nagar. But she seemed to be untraced. With the days going by he became restive to see her. Days went by.

In two months' time he became fully accustomed with Arijit Maity who took the chance to propel him whichever way he found profitable for himself.

The September sky that had shed occasional showers of rain till the afternoon got mostly clear in later afternoon. In the evening Animesh was at Arnab's rented dwelling. "Come on, Animesh, come on in, "Arnab said looking at him smiling and coming out from teaching big kids.

"I see you are teaching," Animesh said. He taught History.

"Yes. You go in and sit. I'll soon be finished," Arnab said.

Animesh walked by the edge of the sitting students in the first room straight into his bedroom and sat on a plastic chair beside his bed. It was a two-roomed dwelling, a part of the old two-storied grey house attached to it. Arnab's rooms had tiles on the roof with a small veranda at the front where he kept his bike.

Animesh waited boringly hearing Arnab teaching and looking around. Down at the floor was a kerosene pump-stove and other utensils, pictures of God and Goddess with calendars under them on the walls, a clothe stand, etc. The single man didn't need many things.

Soon he was finished. He came in. "How are you?" Arnab asked sitting at the edge of the bed.

"Me...? Animesh paused, not knowing what to say. "Just getting on—'cos it has to," he replied. "Tell me about you," he asked Arnab quickly.

"I'm fine. No complaints," Arnab said smiling.

"What about her?" Animesh asked hesitatingly. Arnab looked at his face trying to guess who he meant. Then he got it and smiled at him. "Oh, she?" He asked. Animesh nodded slightly.

"I saw her a few days ago, I mean, last week," Arnab said.

"Did you? Really?" Animesh asked quickly in a rising tone with high curiosity. "How I wished to see her once, but I didn't," he thought to himself. Then he asked him "Where did you see her?" Is she alright?"

"I don't know. I didn't talk to her. She looked like she was alright." Arnab answered. Animesh's enthusiasm got down. "Mmn," he let out the sound without opening his mouth to mean yes.

"Actually I didn't have enough time to talk. At the Bajrang Bali Temple Square, she passed down the other side of the street. When I saw her face, she passed by before I knew. She was on a rickshaw going towards the bus terminus. I didn't call after her. Who knows what she would take it like. I wasn't acquainted with her for long. And she is a young woman. And besides, I heard another piece of news. I wonder if I should break it to you."

"Tell me, what?" Animesh asked impatiently.

"No, I mean it might hurt you." Arnab said fearfully.

Animesh's heart shook at this. He asked anxiously, "Whatever the bad news, tell," he urged.

"Her parents are looking to get her married and have started looking for a groom."

" Animesh's face dried like leaves without water. He managed the blow and asked "What was her reaction? Does she want to marry?"

He seemed anxious. When Arnab said, "She told her parents she wouldn't marry now. She would like to get a job first." Animesh felt comforted for her right decision.

"Good idea. That's what she should do. I wish I could see her. My mind's really whirling," Animesh said earnestly. "I wish I could fly to her like a bird!"

"How come?" Arnab asked. "You don't know where she lives."

"That's the thing to worry about, friend," Animesh said.

"Are you sure she has leant toward you?" Arnab asked.

"I think so," Animesh replied. In fact, her answers to him with her natural smiling and simple jolly way of speaking settled this idea in him. The rest was his blind emotion. Arnab chuckled, and thought he should break the wrong idea that he'd been nourishing in him before he got into trouble.

"By the way," he said, "Just two days ago, ye know, I happened to see Disha, too," he paused. Animesh looked at his face curiously. "Disha? Who?" Animesh asked.

"Disha—the healthy girl, dark complexioned short height, the one who took part in the pantomime, remember?" Arnab said in a questioning tone trying to remind him. "Oh, yes, I remember," said Animesh, "anyway, what about her?"

"She lives on her turf; while talking about her marriage I wanted to pick out something about your affairs—I mean, if she had any feeling towards you." Arnab paused shortly looking at Animesh's face. Here Animesh received a wave of concern. Who knows what he was going to hear from him again. The tone of Arnab's words didn't sound right. Animesh became fearfully curious looking at Arnab's face.

"What did you hear from her, friend? Tell me!" He asked weakly.

"Disha said like this: 'I asked her if she felt anything about Animesh-da.' But she said, Animesh-da is a good person, simple, reticent man staying in his own world, but she also said she had nothing on her mind about him. And she could never go beyond her parents' will.' Then I thought what's Animesh-da has been running after so long?' Disha said like this." Arnab reported.

Animesh's face shrank. He felt it like a hammer banged in his heart. Arnab went on:

"I say, if she can't get down to wet her feet in water, why should you drown yourself in the bottomless waters of the whirlpool and destroy yourself? Forget her. Keep off from her. Come back and live honourably. There's no scarcity of girls yet." Animesh listened to him half-heartedly. They were no welcome words to him. He was struck beneath. He lost his words for the time being. Things seemed to have gone topsy-turvy for him.

Arnab said out, "Never mind that I told you like this, friend," he felt bad having knocked sense into him, "I didn't mean to hurt you."

"Oh, no, no," Animesh said promptly, "What you suggest is alright and precious. But how can I forget her, friend? I have gone too far with her. I have placed and locked her in the deep of my heart's home." He went on. "I can't forget her, Arnab. I can't," he said meltingly. There was emotion in his tone. The soaked eyes reflected the light from his eyes. "I can't concentrate on anything. I can't take anything easy. I'll go crazy, it seems." He looked away in the way of the open door.

"I know how hard it is when you're so gone on her. But still if you try, you can. And you have to. Because I myself was able to come out of such a whirlpool one day in the past." Animesh looked back at Arnab's face. He found somebody to feel his dilemma.

"I'll tell you my story some other day," Arnab said. It was time for him to get out to a student's to give her private coaching.

At the outside gate they held their bicycles in their hands ready to ride away. Don't let yourself destroy, friend." Think of it," Arnab called and rode his bicycle.

Chapter 29

Arijit Maity was a Midnapurian guy (from Midnapore district), a very clever man who knew very well how to insinuate himself into somebody by coaxing and with his special knowledge of tantras to make profit or squeeze money out of somebody. Animesh being a simple, an easy-trusting guy slipped into his trap.

One day in conversation, Mr. Maity asked him his exact date of birth and time. Animesh didn't know them himself. Maity read his palm to tell his fortune. What he told him was scaring.

He said, "You're a guy of Mars's bad influence. You'll get obstructed at any job. Rahu, (the North Node), and Ketu (the South Node) were also in the bad. The Sun-line should have been even better but it is not, the Venus is down which affects the conjugal life of a person very much. Only the Jupiter is somehow in favour of you. The Moon is also in the bad position that causes dangers in water. These stars always do some bad one way or the other. They hinder you from loving and being loved."

That's it. Animesh understood why he was being obstructed at every step he took in finding a way out to the world, in the love affair, in running a business, even in higher education. But what got him most was the hindrance in his love affair at that moment. He ate it up. His face saddened. Maity watched him and went on.

"You do a lot for people, your own folks, but they wouldn't even try to understand you. You'll love people honestly; without pretension, but they won't, because of these enemy stars."

Maity also warned him about his movement on the way. "Being the Mars down, and the Rahu against, you might face a street mishap. Be careful while you are on the move. These bad stars need to be treated," Maity added, noticing how easily he succeeded in getting him in his way.

Animesh thought fearfully staring at his face. "Then what fortune have I been carrying?" he asked. What he always ran after and was anxious for was any possibility of crossing the Atlantic. He asked, "Isn't there anything about my going abroad?"

Maity checked his palm again pressing around the hypothenar of his palm above his wrist and shook his head. "There isn't anything like that," he said still examining his palm. "The moon helps you go away from the country. But it is affected by the Mars and Saturn. There is no sign of the moon in such a position to send you abroad." He looked at Animesh's face. "You see, most of your resulting stars were in the bad. Besides, the enemy stars worked against at the same time and you were hindered from being succeeded. The Jupiter is always in your favour and sometimes the Sun backs you to get over or to escape with small harms."

Animesh was now very much dejected. He found from his past failures that Maity was right in most cases and he trusted him, which went more in favour of him than Animesh himself.

"There's no love from people! No co-operation from people! Hard-earned money wouldn't be saved! No peace in the family! Even, no success in love!" Animesh said out surprised. "Then what the hell of the good is there in my fortune? What's the worth carrying a failed life like this? Just living like street dogs? Oh dear God! I can't stand all these misjudgements. Give me a spare, God!" Animesh spilled his pent up sorrow and anger. Maity chuckled looking down at him spitting out against his fortune and consoled him. "Why worry? There are ways to treat them for the betterment. Don't break down so easily," he tried to reassure him.

This man didn't take any fee from him but he made it up the other way around. He had him offer away five-hundred and one rupees for worshipping his own tantric Goddess in the name of working out the good for Animesh, dispelling troubles that might come around. He didn't just stop there. He had him buy himself a few costly stones. In spite of being tight-fisted, he bought them, certainly, he was hexed by his tantra. He no longer thought of moving out to a rented room. Animesh already had a pearl, a red coral but he said they were not of good quality. Wearing them would even be more harmful. In fact, to all astrologers stones worn by a client would be of bad quality, no matter how costly it would be or how good. He presented himself to be the real well-wisher to him like an angel from God in heaven. Animesh blew up half of his money of his salaries on the Amway business. It was another misfortune. And nobody would know how hard it had been for him to spend so much money on the jewellery stones. The only privillege that he had was that he didn't have to give money to his brother to support the six-member family at home. The small business of his father's under the two brothers ran the family. That's why people of his turf and elsewhere would reasonably think that Animesh's money was being piled up into a hill. But, only he knew where he had been.

Chapter 30

The words from Maity about his failures in his first true love whirled in his mind—the more he thought of it, the more he grew anxious. It had been two months since he came back to Burdwan. He even couldn't take a distant look at her even for once. He thought of it and sighed out deeply.

After tea in the evening Maity went out on his business matter for about one and a half hours. Animesh was in the room. He read the letter that he had written for about ten days. He had already made a lot of changes in it, added new sentences and rhymes. It was intended for her. By hook or by crook he would have to reach his last ever message to her. Now he read it through to give it another check. It seemed to be all right now. Writing is a peculiar thing; that is, the more you check, the more changes it deserves. While reading it, the face of Anamika floated before his eyes. He opened the photo file and took the photos of her. He got buried in thought of her while gazing at them. The doors of the room were just pushed to as usual because opposite the room were other rooms in a row on the ground floor and up to the second floor. This room was extended from the main building. So, people moving about the door would be able to peek in.

Animesh lay over on his knees and arms, and dozed off with photos of her beside his head, his hands around one close-up photo of her and the photo file half open next to him by the wall. While staring at the photos, he didn't know when he'd fallen in a drowsy state.

Just as Maity stepped in pushing the door, Animesh startled out of his drowsiness and scrambled up quickly to sitting; guiltily, feeling embarrassed of his silly blind emotion. Maity smiled quietly and patted on his back sympathetically. "There! There! Poor chap!" He said soothingly. "It's all right. Don't take it hard, man."

He sat on the edge of his own bed facing Animesh looking down at him feelingly. "I know how you feel about her. How greatly you love her. But what is pitiful is that she never knew you. She didn't even try to know you how much you love her. Where you have placed her, and she wouldn't know unless you can let her know. I can't bear to see you in such miseries."

Animesh was going to pack up the photos shyly in the file when Maity held out his hand for them. He handed them to him. He stared at them keenly like a great artist. "She's alright; looking like a good girl—polite, intelligent, but she's arrogant of her beauty," he explained. "However, almost all beautiful girls hold and indulge conceit in them," he added.

"I didn't see arrogance in her," Animesh advocated for her. "I saw her for about a year in college."

Nobody would allow criticism against the one they loved wholeheartedly. Maity remembered the saying: 'Love makes people blind'. But he didn't say a word. He didn't want to hurt the one who had already been hurt and weak from his painful love.

Instead, he softly said, "You wouldn't know it just by looking at somebody outwardly. I can only know with my special power," he said proudly. His special power meant to be his astrological power and tantric influence. Animesh didn't say anything to his pride.

"Anyway, except for that point she could be a good match for you," he said to soothe him. "Just by worshipping like this you can't succeed but ruin yourself. Why not go over to her and tell her all about how you adore her, how you care for her?" He suggested him wisely.

"How can I go? I don't know where she lives." Animesh answered helplessly.

"People find out new planets in the vast endless space! You can't find her in this small place! If you wanna have something so badly, you must find a way out," he tried to encourage him.

"Don't you see her anywhere while you're on your way to and back?"

"No, I didn't see her yet. I always keep my eyes peeled for her on the way."

Maity handed him the pictures back. Animesh slipped them into the envelope and then put them back in the photo file.

"Which area does she live?" he asked, his hand was on his knee. He was still sitting at the edge of his bed hanging his legs down.

"Somewhere around Kanchan-Nagar, I heard," Animesh answered.

"Kanchan-Nagar—means towards the North-West," he said softly gesturing at the direction.

"Good." he said confidently. "I'll see to it," he reassured. "Don't worry."

So saying, he stood up for a change of his garments. Animesh felt a bit reassured because Maity had lots of people in the know from his business. "Don't worry," he repeated. "I'll see to it."

Chapter 31

Sometime in the long past, some great man of great philosophy made this proverb: Where there is a will there is a way. This great saying sometimes somewhere goes true with some people but not for always, not for everybody. All other wills of Animesh ended in failure but this one came true.

He was able to find a way to Anamika's home after two months' indomitable efforts. By this time, the letter intended for her was fully complete with the latest corrections. This was the first time ever he had written such a letter for a girl and it was the longest ever letter he wrote ever in his life. It had four A4-sized pages hand-written on one side of each page. They were joined end to end with gum and it looked like an unrolled scroll that used to be sent by a king to another king with messages in the long past. When the letter was folded into a suitable size to fit it in a medium-sized envelope, it swelled like a flat money purse of a woman.

In this longest letter, he tried to spill out his heart-felt feeling and liking and love for her and wanted her to realize it before she decided differently. It was the first time ever in his life he fell in love with a girl, and it was with Anamika, his love was true, honest, and solid, and everlasting. While expressing his emotional feeling there came a few short poems of his own composition and some quotes from great men in the suitable places with sober choice of words and language.

Today was the day. He had to go through a slight palpitation inside his chest all day which increased as the time came closer in the afternoon; he was going to meet her. Every so often, while working, chatting or staying idle, this matter bobbed up in his head with a cold wave through his heart. He anxiously thought what was going to happen—what reaction it would spark or how she would react— in his favour or against, what he would speak to her—how he'd hand the letter to her, and many more things.

In fact, he thought of seeing her so seriously that it seemed to be no less than an important interview at some grand company for a decent job. What he didn't do was he didn't get dressed decent or smart enough like that for a big interview. He was a simple country boy without style, living a simple easy-go life without being stuffed up of conceit. He mostly spent his leisure time reading and listening to music or foreign radio programmes. He believed and followed his English guru Mr. Pradip De's one piece of evaluation of life. He'd once said: "It's no worth brightening yourself outwardly with clothes and style to show the world while your inside is dark from lack of real education, good humanism. It is worth brightening your inside with real education, high education, deep knowledge and wisdom and real humanity. If you think a lot of your outside brightness, you waste lots of your precious time and good money in it, which will cause scarcity of money and time for your inside brightness. Rather, you should dress up properly just according to what the situation deserves. That's all."

Animesh wore a light yellow full-sleeved shirt tucked in and a pair of greyish-blue trousers with a black belt on. His hair was brushed plainly parted above his left ear and wore his glasses for distant vision. He didn't treat his face or use perfume.

It was a good five kilometres to Kanchan-nagar from downtown Burdwan. It was a distant part of Burdwan town with a touch of a village ambience with many trees and plants, and lots of open land for cultivation. The road was a little higher than the grassy surface on both sides. Mostly one-storey houses and two-storey houses were seen with enough space at the front or by their sides suitable for growing vegetables or flowers. The air was fresher than the air in Burdwan. A little way farther around the south was the sluice gate on the Banka River to control and propel its water for irrigation. The place looked so great with many date palms, and wild trees and plants surrounding it. Arnab drove his bike and he had to ask around to find out the house they wanted.

His bike screeched to a halt by the side of the road and looked up at the door. Animesh swung his leg over the back of the seat to get off the bike and then Arnab followed suit. While he stood the bike on its side stand, Animesh took a quick look around. This place of Kanchan-Nagar seemed rather densely populated with closely set-up old-fashioned houses with small windows and two-panelled doors. Houses were on both sides of the road. It was dusty and full of pits.

Animesh looked at the brown-painted, entrance-door panels. The colour of them faded in many years. The letter box on it showed U.C. Sen, Jay Prakash Malobyo Street, Kanchan-Nagar, Burswan 713202. The one-storied simple old house was situated on a higher gradient of a slightly slopped surface. Animesh took the small opaque polythene bag out of the big poly-bag and then the envelope out of it and held it in his right hand. He felt the thumping of his fast beating heart behind his chest, his throat dried and he began to swallow hard—'what's going to happen in a moment!' he wondered. He tried to look normal but anxiety and fear ringed him almost all over. He put the envelope back into the polythene bag.

Arnab pressed the calling bell; it was bad. Then he gave a knock on the door. There was no sign of reaction to the knock, though clanks of utensils came from inside. He knocked again; this time a bit louder. Arnab stepped back a little from the door and waited looking at the door, then sideways at the street, Animesh standing beside him uneasily.

"Someone's at the door." A female voice called. "Kolmee, go 'n get the door."

"Who is it?" said another female voice that sounded sweet and young as she was approaching. It seemed to be that familiar voice to Animesh that sounded like that of wind chimes. It was Anamika's voice. He recognized it. He was pleased and thanked God in mind—she was at home. Hope rose in him along with anxiety.

"Who is it?" she called again.

"Me, Arnab," he answered. His answer went right across the closed wooden doors. Now they could hear the thongs scraping on the rough concrete surface. They looked at the door. The doors opened apart. It was Anamika there.

To her surprise, she saw Animesh standing next to Arnab with his hands hanging down loosely with a small poly-bag hanging from his hand. Her face seemed to shrink right away and face turned blue and angry that Animesh didn't notice. He took a shy heartfelt look at the long-cherished sweetest face of her so intently but carefully so as not be looking silly to her. At the same time he had to shift his concentration to how Arnab was managing the unexpected situation and what she answered. And above all the villain of tension in him was active in full. He tried nervously to evaluate the overall situation.

They had expected to be asked in for a while but, to their surprise, she didn't even talk to Arnab with the minimum courtesy. She somehow made them feel it with the way she talked and with her grim face that she was rather annoyed being visited. "You're here?" she asked in a surprised tone of voice.

"Yes, we're here," Arnab replied casually moving his hands dramatically. "We were going back home from a friend of mine this way." He gestured at the north up the way. "So, I kind of thought of swinging by your home. That's it. And I didn't hear from you since we left college. That's it," he explained sensing the situation. The self-composed impromptu answer didn't sound natural even to his own ears. She was still uncharacteristically unenthusiastic.

"Anyway, how are you?" Arnab asked to turn the situation the other way to make it light.

"Fine," she replied in short.

"Are you getting ready for the next SSC?"

"Not yet." Her lips parted and closed.

"The results are said to be out in November," he said again.

"I heard so. Let it come out. I'm not in a hurry." Her cold words seemed to be forced out of her mouth. The two guys well understood it.

"You can start the SSC preparation." Arnab suggested casually.

She didn't answer. By now they got to know they shouldn't stick around here anymore. Animesh's mood and enthusiasm was smashed up like a skyscraper demolished by detonators and he didn't dare ask her if the photos of the annual function were all right, or if she wanted some copies of other photos of her. How could he dare give the letter to her? His heart sank, his face turned blue, and inside his body it shivered radiating heat from his body. It was the biggest defeat and greatest failure since the B. Ed session. Sweat had already started streaming down his back under his shirt. He closed his eyes for a tiny moment from the pressure of hopelessness thinking, "Oh God!"

"All right, nice meeting you after a long time," Arnab said in courtesy with a subtle touch of irony in the end, "Stay lucky." She didn't react to it either.

No sooner had they turned around than the doors banged shut behind them. While Arnab was turning the bike around, Animesh's head leant down forward from deep thought and anxiety. "What the hell happened?" He asked himself. He could hardly trust his eyes what he saw right before his own eyes. Neither of them could believe they would be treated so nastily. She didn't prove the basic etiquette and courtesy of a normal family. Apparently, it looked inhumane to them because it was beyond their expectations but reasonably, she was right at her position; any other person in the same situation would probably consider it right. She had no way other than this.

Chapter 32

Arnab turned his bike and started the engine with a soft spatter. Animesh climbed up on the pillion seat; they started for home.

The first ever love, the deepest ever emotion of Animesh and the long hard labour for the longest ever love letter—all turned out to be the worst ever tragedy in the twinkle of an eye which was even beyond a dream in sleep only because of the lack of his knowledge and experiences of the practical world. Like an immature fruit tried to ripen in calcium carbide against nature would be spoiled up, it happened so to his love as well.

They were going back down the same way they had come. Their faces were blue, and anyone observing carefully could see it. They didn't speak down the way back for minutes. Now Arnab said out, "Unexpected." A moment later he said again, Anyway, what happened, happened for the best."

Arnab stopped short to buy a cigarette from a kiosk on the road. "Will you have a smoke?" Arnab asked him. "No, thanks, I won't. I don't do drugs," he replied. Arnab put the cigarette in his chest pocket and started again. A little way ahead, he halted on a bridge of the Banka River from where the green beauty of the sluice gates was seen. The water was turbid from the monsoon rain flowing slowly in circles.

It was not a busy road at all. A few people were on the way, and vehicles were still less. They got off the bike. Arnab left the bike on its stand and stepped onto the raised sidewalk of the bridge. They stood facing each other with the parapet behind them.

"I don't usually smoke but now I feel like smoking one," Arnab said. "My head feels pretty jammed." He put the Wills Filter between his lips. He stopped a middle-aged man in a dhoti for a match and lit it and stepped back onto the raised sidewalk. Now they stood face to face with the parapet beside them, their hands on the parapet. He dragged on it twice before he spoke again. "What do you think of what happened today, Animesh?" He asked letting the smoke out of his mouth. Animesh had already felt that the painful situation would be raised now.

"I wonder what's this that's just happened and why. My head's spinning," Animesh answered slowly from hesitation. "I'm dumbfounded. I'm shocked." His head turned sideways.

"I'd, however, guessed somewhat like this might come, but I couldn't think it'd be that bad and she could behave so strangely, like this. She seemed to be discontented to see you right at her door." He explained drawing at the cigarette. "I think her parents warned her against any affairs because they were looking for a groom and she was reluctant to marry right now."

"Who know?" Animesh said plainly.

After a few more puffs from the cigarette, Arnab cast an unsatisfied, curious look at it. Something was not right. He took another puff and felt it the same way; unsatisfied. He threw it over the parapet into the river. Animesh saw it fall onto the turbid water and being carried away by the slow current.

Arnab started again. "Animesh, what happened to you, in fact, is one-sided love," Arnab said seriously. "You've taken her into the core of your heart. You've been crazy for her, but it is obvious now that she has nothing of you in her. She didn't even try to check how much you've offered yourself up to her. Maybe, she's has given her heart to somebody else."

He spat out across the parapet into the river from the bitter taste of the cigarette and wiped his mouth with the handkerchief.

He looked back at his face. "This one-sided love, one-sided trust is much too dangerous. Nobody can realize it unless they have been in it. It's like running after a mirage in the deep of the desert and finding nothing in the end and getting lost for keeps finding no way back."

Animesh listened to him silently, sometimes looking at his face, and sometimes looking away past him at the field or down at the

Banka's turbid water flowing away circling slowly. His head didn't work. He couldn't take anything practical or philosophical words at that moment.

"Animesh, I'm scared of that thing—the non-existent thing. I suggest you get back while there is time. Forget her. You'll live then. I already told you the same thing."

Animesh's look came back to Arnab's face and his lips suddenly parted and closed again as if he wanted to speak. But he didn't have a chance to speak while fumbling for words before Arnab spoke again.

"Don't make any more blunders, friend," Arnab urged and held Animesh's hand earnestly. "As a true friend, Animesh, I'm telling you with the blue heaven above and the life-saving water underneath, save yourself. There's a long way to go, lots of things to do, lots to give to the society as a teacher. You've got your mother at home. Think of her."

Animesh started to say, "Please, try to..." Arnab stopped short to let Animesh speak.

"Try to feel it my way. It's just words from your lips, but what I feel is in the deep of my heart. Arnab, I'm undone. I'm already lost in her desert. I can see she's a desert but still I can't forget her and come back. I lost my way there long before. I can't do anything else," he said meltingly turning his back on to the parapet and looking away over the bridge.

"I understand your plight, friend, but still, you're still in the wrong." He urged, "Listen, listen to me good—you can, I say you can. From the bottom of my heart, I feel you can come out of that hell. Man can do anything if he wills. Be strong. Be determined. You shall succeed. I'm with you to help you. You just help me." He took in a short breath.

"You've got an honourable government job. You're handsome enough. You've got good education, knowledge and wisdom. Why should you admit defeat? Look, dames are dames. They will come flooding in with a snap of your finger. Let them." He tried to encourage him into the practical life.

Animesh was confused. He kept silent only looking at the trees across the Banka River up at the sluice gates while Arnab looked up at his poor face reading it.

"I'll remember your words and try," Animesh said but weakly.

Chapter 33

A lot of things happened since last year's September. He had the great storm blowing through his mind. His health broke down; his weight was lost by about four kilograms. He couldn't keep his word to Arnab about forgetting her either, his everyday work was affected. He was in a fix from both ways—he couldn't withdraw himself from her indomitable pull. On the contrary, he didn't have a way to get closer to her. It was such a strange situation. By brooding his days were passing by. He often thought in his loneliness: If she'd turned up by some miracle and tell him she was sorry for that day's behaviour! In the next moment he thought it was silly of him to expect like this.

This morning he woke up pleased. He had a sweet dream—she turned up to him at the station of Katwa, all of a sudden, telling him: "Very hard way I had my parents agreed. We shouldn't be late for the registry; do something right today." Animesh was on top of the world at that moment to hear her say so. His broad smile played all over his face. "That's just great," he said. "You did a great job." He took a breath. "Yes, certainly, we shouldn't be late at all." They started walking to find a wedding office in the town. They looked for the office crazily but they couldn't find it out.

Suddenly he woke up from tension and regretted to have his sleep broken untimely with the dream incomplete. Anyway, all day long the dream came up in his mind and felt him good. His expectation had a boost like the spring tide in a dry river. For about a week he felt nice to think of the dream and wished it'd come true!

He couldn't help telling it to Arijit Maity. He smiled and said, "A dream is a dream. All the same if it comes true, I'll be more pleased than anybody else. But still it won't be wise to hold on to the dream and keep losing your precious life." The impact of the dream waned after a month but still he waited if she changed her mind. She would come into his mind repeatedly like an advertisement would come round over and over again on the electronic board.

Mr. Maity and Arnab still convinced him to come out of it, on the other hand, Animesh's folks constantly convinced him into finding out a pretty bride to marry her. In the mean time his relatives took him to visit one or two brides but whoever he met, he looked for Anamika in them and compared them with her, but he didn't find any similarities. He couldn't get ahead.

When days were passing by this way, there happened something terrible to him that he never ever experienced or expected.

Chapter 34

Maity and Animesh both had their supper early because, Prokash Chakraborty, the home-delivery man of meals had come early and told them to eat early. He had to attend a wedding reception. He went up the other floors of the hotel to deliver a few meals there. He used to take the four-box meal carrier with him after their eating for the next day's meal. Maity washed his boxes and Animesh washed his, set them in the holding frame and put them down on the floor next to their plank bedsteads. Animesh started reading the story book again before he went to sleep: Narayan Sanyal's Bisswaas Ghaatok, which could be entitled in English as 'The Traitor', about the invention of the first atom bomb and dropping it on Japan and the trafficking of the formulae into another country from the Manhattan Project. He had been reading it bit by bit for about a week. Suddenly his Motorola mobile trilled next to him on the bed. He looked down at the screen. It was from an unknown number. He took it up and pressed down the button.

"Hello!" he said coldly.

"Hello! A female voice said. "Are you Animesh sir?" she asked.

"Yes," replied Animesh.

"Sir, I'm from Bantir—Purnima's mother," she identified herself.

"Anyway, what's the matter?" he asked.

"Sir, I'm in a great danger."

"In a great danger!" he exclaimed in wonder.

"Yes, Purnima has taken poison—pesticide," she said. "She's in Burdwan Hospital." Her voice broke.

"Poison!" he exclaimed in surprise. "Why? Why did she do so?" He asked.

"We don't know," she answered. Maity was smoking a cigarette after supper. He became aware and curious when he heard about poison. He looked at Animesh's face curiously.

"When did it happen?" asked Animesh.

She said, "Yesterday."

"How's she now?" Animesh asked plainly.

"She's serious, doctor said." With a short pause, she said, "Sir, are you in Burdwan?"

"Yes," he replied in short.

"Sir, she wants to see you once. She spoke about you," the woman said. Her words sounded a bit different to him. "She wants to see you once, sir." She repeated.

"Wants to see me!" Why?" he was surprised even more.

"Will you please come over and see her once?" she requested.

"Let me see when I can make time," he said hesitantly. Hospital was a place he always wanted to avoid for the odd mixed tangy stink and the gloomy ambience all over. He would have nausea in that environment.

"Please, try to come, sir," she urged again.

"I'll see to it," he said and cut it off and put it down next to him annoyingly. He looked up at Maity who had been watching him speak to her.

"It's a hassle," Animesh said. "A girl student of my school has taken poison," he reported to Maity.

"I heard," said Mr Maity. "Do you wanna visit her?"

"Yes, I told her mother so," he replied honestly.

"Are you off your head?" Maity said in a scolding mood. Animesh got confused, not understanding its graveness. He looked up at his face thoughtfully.

"Who knows what the affair is behind it?" Maity asked. Animesh began to realize it. He looked thoughtful.

"Did she ever tell you she loved you? Or behaved in a way that indicated love?"

"No, never. I'm her teacher. Why should she think that way?" Animesh said reasonably.

"There's no telling what can happen to whom and how," Maity said, "Then what was she like to you?"

"She was a very obedient student. She respected me kind of too much in comparison to other girl students." Animesh explained in short.

"Many a time it happens that someone respecting too much or showing too much obedience slips into a love affair." Maity explained.

"Then why did she take poison?" Animesh asked.

"Maybe, she thought she wouldn't get a room in you, or maybe she played the love game with another guy who kicked her off after he'd knocked her up. Who knows? Anything could happen."

Animesh's head bent down from a growing anxiety sitting cross-legged on the bed, his hands beside him supporting his weight.

"Don't worry. Things will come off alright. I'll see it in my meditation," he comforted him. Animesh nodded his head weakly but anxiety began to rise in him. He leant his head gravely.

Chapter 35

The next day in the evening the two guys were having tea and brown-baked bread when Maity asked, "Did you get any information about that girl from school?"

"Nothing much, only that she took poison and not out of danger yet," Animesh answered. "They hope she'll be alright."

"Hoping is something, and the ultimate result is something else. We all can hope and always should hope for the better but fortune defines everything that either goes along with our expectation or against, but most often goes opposite to our hopes," Maity said wisely. Animesh nodded to his reasons and the reality with anxiety. "Did you find anything about her?" Animesh asked. Yes, I'm gonna tell you," he said, "Have your tea first." His graveness was noticeable.

After they'd had tea, Maity began. "I saw about the case in my meditation last night and again at noon."

Animesh concentrated his attention on his face deeply. "The girl is in a critical situation. Maybe she's slipped into unconsciousness. I wonder how much she told her folks about you, but I found that they've got a big conspiracy against you." Maity paused for a moment looking down at his face seriously.

"Conspiracy! Against me!" Animesh fell from the sky to hear it. His jaw dropped. It sounded like a bolt from the blue.

"Why should they be down after me? What's the reason? I did nothing, no wrong," he said confusedly with emphasis.

"You did nothing—so you say, but what if she's spoken to her parents something else?" Maity asked apprehensively. "A girl or a woman can do anything at will. The law is in their favour, not yours. They can trap somebody anytime anywhere if they want. Not only that, they have put on a harmful sangoma against you to hex you—either to get her married to you and convert you to their religion or to squeeze out a big amount of money with a slander on your reputation using her scandal."

"How will they plant her pregnancy on me? It deserves to be proved through examination," Animesh asked reasonably.

"You're right. You will get the chance later and if she survives. But before that there is a lot of time for all of it to spread out in the media and on people's lips."

"Oh my God!" He mumbled under his breath and resettled himself on his seat, looking downward. It began to shiver in his body now spreading out through his body.

"Besides, the political party will stand by them. Above all, it also touched the religious sensitivity. Will it be too hard a thing to change the results of the examination that you are talking about emphatically?" With a short pause he said, "Only political influence."

Animesh's face dried and shrunk. He became aware that it was the communist rule. Those places were the strongholds of the communist power. He knew how ruthless communists could be.

"Oh, dear me!" he blurted out bending forward and covered his face in his hands.

Maity went on. "They will try to succeed over you in all the ways. They know a teacher's dignity is high enough in the society. You'll be easily made a scapegoat with a threat of dignity-loss."

He felt that his throat came drying from inside up to his tongue. He gulped down several times. As Maity spoke, he observed serious changes across his face. And he spoke more. "A scandal spreads like wild fires. Whoever will hear of it will stand by the victim—the girl, not by you."

"A big scandal, and that too, with a student! All will be splashed out in the newspapers! On TV! If I'm arrested even for a few days, I'll be suspended from school and then I might even lose my job! All people in here, in my school, out there in my hometown will get to know! Oh my God! What the hell is this? How could I ever show my face!" All these thoughts ran riot through his head, his eyes closed, his head bent down: "Reporters are hovering around Burdwan town. Just with a smell of it, they will rush down to the spot."

Animesh felt as if he lost his weight as he was sitting cross-legged loosely on the hard plank bedstead, his hands behind him supporting his weight.

"You don't need to worry right now. Let's wait one day more and watch things," Maity tried to console him. "While I'm here with you, I'll try my best to protect you like an elder brother does for his younger brother."

"That's very kind of you," Animesh said in gratefulness," Please, do something."

"I need to do a grand Yognya that is a *Vedic Sacrifice* for you. It'll be costly," he said seriously. Animesh wondered about its costs apprehensively. "How much could it cost?" He asked fearfully. Maity gave an estimate: "More or less two thousand."

"Quite a lot." Animesh said suppressing his exclamation, his face got down again from thought. It was urgent and inevitable; he wasn't supposed to be tight-fisted about spending what it deserved to tide him over the trouble.

"I told you it'd be costly. But it's important for you at this moment according to the situation. Think of it. If you can't carry it all at a time, pay me the half now, and I'll tide you over. You pay off the rest later." He offered.

"That's better," he said.

"Where will you do the Vedic sacrifice?" Animesh asked.

"It was to have been best done at Kamakkhya but there's not enough time. I can't reach there before the full moon." Kamakkhya was in Assam in Eastern India, the best place of tantras in the whole of India.

"Then?" Animesh wondered.

"Then it's better done at Nimtala Grand Crematorium. It was in Calcutta. It will take a very long time," He continued. "One more thing," he paused, "by the time you may happen to be coming across a snake or that on your way. Be careful you don't happen to fall too close to it or step on it. It'll be very dangerous for you then."

Animesh looked up at his face more fearfully than curiously, "Above all, snakes!" He muttered. "Why snakes?"

"I'd already told you, they set a great sangoma after you. He let out a hexed snake after you."

"Is it possible at all?" He expressed doubt.

"If you don't trust me, you fight your own battle if you can. It's no use getting me involved in it. You have no idea about black tantra or necromancy. You don't know its power. Everything is possible in it," he snapped.

Here the tone of his words scared him. "Oh, my God!" Animesh exclaimed. "What the hell is it happening to me?" He said from burning anger inside. "I never did nothing to nobody nowhere, why the fuck should they be down after me?" He spat in rage. Maity watched that his temper frayed from bewilderment.

"It happens in the most developed, highest class of animal on the earth—with humans. You don't always have to do any wrong to them. Some dogs bark at or bite people for no reason. Some snakes chase people to bite with no wrong done to them. Why? It's just a special dirty characteristic of some animals who walk on two feet to reap the pleasure out of dragging somebody into trouble or causing them to suffer somehow." Animesh happened to remember his English guru Mr. Pradip De say the same thing one day in the evening when sitting around on the platform bench of Katwa Railway Station in their outdoor practical class when some well-dressed guys taunted them for speaking English between themselves. Mr De had evaluated them this way like dogs barking at them for no reason.

After a long talk about it, Maity asked him to sleep freely, once again reassuring him of fighting it off to the end for him.

The night passed. The sun got up. Animesh didn't feel like getting up from laziness and weakness out of deep concern. He took a brief look out of the corners of his eyes that Maity was in meditation mode in front of Goddess Kali. He still lay on with his eyes closed. But suddenly he felt uneasy to lie in bed like that while Maity was working hard for him. So, he got up and off the bed and shaped up the bedding to its place at the head of the bedstead and went out to the sink with his brush. He did the morning washes with a heavy head and concerned mind. His legs felt too heavy and his movement was not as agile as before. He didn't turn the radio on for the news, not the cassette player to listen to his favourite songs for two days. He let out a deep sigh from time to time remembering God to protect him. He asked himself when the horrible terror-days would be over, how the next few days would pass away.

"Anything more out of the meditation?" Animesh asked while having tea. Makhom had brought the morning tea.

"At midnight, too, I was in meditation. What came was still critical. They may have done an FIR in the mean time so that the case would be started right away in case she died."

On hearing this, Animesh swallowed hard as if his throat was squeezed by something. The shiver that went through his body since that day was still on; or rather it was on the rise. He was drinking tea sort of forcefully; it didn't seem to get down his throat. He was about to take another sip at the earthen cup but the cup stopped short near his lips. He put it down. "Then how's the girl?" he asked.

"Still critical, probably she has deteriorated," Maity replied sipping at his cup.

"Will she die then?" He asked fearfully. From deep concern, it felt him as if he didn't have his mass of the body; but as light as cotton. He was sitting with his legs down from the plank bedstead, his hands beside him as if to prop himself up from falling. He felt he was swaying slightly from the pounding of his heart.

Arijit Maity dropped the earthen cup into the litterbin. "Why break down so easily?" He injected guts into him. "I'll try my best to protect you. Get over just this day. Tomorrow I will do everything possible."

It didn't reassure him enough. Sitting the same way, he put his hands behind him in support and leaned backwards a little, his head down, the half-drunk tea left beside him. He felt too scared now to go to school for fear of being caught by her folks on the way. Even the cops might be looking for him. What a terrible situation!

Chapter 36

It was better for him not to have gone out today. Still he did. He was in the middle place by a window of the bus to Shyamsunder. He shrunk to the sidewall and half leant, his head slightly down in a way so as not to be seen easily but it wouldn't look odd to people either; if anybody of the girl was up on the bus! He wished he had closed the window but he didn't; passengers might object to it. He wished the bus had been crowded to shadow him from being seen, but it hadn't been. He wished that the bus had started right away so that the girl's folks wouldn't be able to catch it at the last moment to get back home from the hospital after the night stay there, but it did take its time. He got silently restive often stealing a look around or at the passengers getting on the bus.

Good luck on him, the journey was safe. Getting off the bus, he hurried into Didi's Hotel for a set meal. He'd always sit on the outer side near the front of the hotel. Today he sat inside, on the farthest tip of one of the two, long, empty benches opposite to each other in the room. This hotel had earthen wall and thatched roofs in a sharp slope. He had been eating here every morning since he joined the school. "Too far from the front today?" asked the elder of the two sisters because both the benches were all empty.

"Yes, I sat kind of absent-mindedly here and didn't feel like moving over," Animesh answered hiding the truth. He wished heartily none of the girls' folks would come in until he went out and notice him eating from the extended part of the hotel room, because many passengers would sit on the small bench of the extended part for tea or deep-fried chops or waiting for the bus towards Golapnagar, Natu Haripur.

The didi gave him a stainless-steel flat dish with a plate of sal leaves in it and served rice, some fried potato, some watery lentil dal and a mixed-veg curry, for the set meal and an omelette on order for which he had to pay extra. After he'd started eating, he felt couldn't eat. Extreme fear was getting him around. He thought he shouldn't have got in here for a meal today, instead, he ought to have eaten some dry food from some shop. Anyway there was no way to leave now.

He finished eating hurriedly. After he'd had a wash outside the hotel under the small bokul tree at the frontage, he sat on the empty outside bench and waited for anyone of his colleagues passing by on the motorbike. He used to go to school on one of his colleague's bikes. He needed to get off here as soon as could be. He was so tensed that he looked down restively at his watch quite often. He didn't sit and wait on the inside bench lest he should fail to signal a passing-by colleague to take him. The earlier anybody would arrive, the better for him. He wondered why Mr. Sarkar, who always went to school the earliest was late today.

Suddenly he thought some guys were watching him like informers would do. His finger had already started pricking at nails of his other hand and looked to the bazar-way that his colleagues would come from. Only today they seemed to be getting late especially when he needed one of them so badly to get into school. Time seemed to tick away too slowly; a minute seemed to be an hour to him now. It was then Animesh noticed that two motorbikes with one rider on the pillion seat came from his school-way, slowed down in front of the hotel and cast a brief look at the hotel where he was sitting and then turned around and drove away down the road they'd come. That did it. Animesh's eyes goggled from fear for a second. "Oh shit!" he thought and sucked in his breath sharply, "just what I'd apprehended!" He startled inwardly like a deer when it suddenly felt a lion behind it on the prowl. A sharp wave of a cold blow passed across his heart. His blood came chilling through his veins. Everybody knew that teachers went to school around this time down this way.

"The two bikers must have discovered me and turned back to inform them of my presence here to ring him up. God! What can do now? Why ever in hell did I come out to school today in such a situation?" he thought to himself and repented badly. He felt his face reflecting uneasy warmth of great tension.

He considered that it was best for him to go back to Burdwan right away. He needed a quick concrete decision now. He nervously walked over to the bus-stop pondering, only fifteen meters from the hotel but couldn't wait there for the bus to Burdwan lest someone got off the bus from Burdwan would easily notice him. So, he walked a little further towards the market area—the main bus stop of Shyamsunder for an up going bus, but stopped short again a little way ahead at the side of the road, because the market would be more crowded where someone of her folks might be. He was in a dilemma. Standing by the road nervously, he was in two minds again; whether he would go back to Burdwan or to school—he would have to decide before a Burdwan-bus or a colleague came. Nervousness rose higher and higher. A quarter of a minute went by, half a minute went by, more moments went by. The pricking at the nails was still going on. Nail tips got short from pricking them unnoticed. He couldn't decide yet. It was then Mr. Som, one of his colleagues, came on his faded golden bike and stopped to a halt in front of him to get him. Animesh couldn't tell him he was going back. He climbed up on the pillion seat behind him sort of unwillingly.

The bike ran with the soft vroom towards the north to the school by Didi's hotel, and by the police station which was another big spot for his concern. With rows of small trees and ditches on both sides of the road, through the open farming land the bike ran. He kept himself straight behind him so as not to be easily noticed. Mr. Som, who was handsome with a manly appearance, slightly taller and wider than him drove on without speaking a word. Animesh didn't speak because he was buried in worries of the forbidding.

"Did I do another blunder to have had a ride for school? Is something worse on the way? Or in school?" He asked himself. The more the bike went ahead, the worrier he became and clucked in regret repeatedly which Mr. Som didn't hear over the vroom. His weary eyes were open if anybody was looking for him. He wished that the few hours in school would pass away good!

Chapter 37

The school hours passed through deep concern but without being bothered. Usually he spoke a lot but today he spoke far less, and sat quietly on his seat and tried not to show impression of worries on his face. Some guys were curious about his reticence, he said he wasn't feeling well.

From Curzon Gate bus stop, he hurried through the alleyway up to his room instead of going around the main street. He pushed the door open and saw Maity sitting cross-legged on the colourful tapestry rag on his plank bedstead worshipping Goddess. Animesh silently put down his bag on the bed and sat down on the edge of his bed for a while. Then he went out to the bathroom to wash the stickiness on the body from the growing summer.

Maity was still worshipping. He dressed up and sat down quietly watching him and waited till it was over, his heart was heavy. The sweet smell of the burning incense sticks filled the room. He watched him bow down to Goddess with deep respect, get off the tapestry rag, folded it up and put it back. He was wearing a saffron dhoti and a white cotton vest for worshipping. He changed them for his normal trousers and shirt. "So you're back," he said sitting on the edge of his bed, "Good."

Animesh nodded, "Yes," he said under his breath.

"I've been waiting for you," he said. "Did you have any trouble in school?" He asked.

"No," Animesh replied. "But..."

"But?" he asked quickly looking eagerly at his face.

Ahindra told the whole situation out there at the hotel.

"You luckily escaped, "he said, "They won't let you off so easily." They're trying to catch you."

"Are they? Really?" Animesh asked tremulously.

"Yes. They're just waiting for the ultimate result of her treatment. If she dies, they'll swarm over you," Maity said which sounded like a deeper warning.

"How's the girl?" Did you find anything more in the meditation?" He asked fearfully.

"What I found is she's still in critical condition, probably steady, not much responding to treatment." He paused shortly. "Actually poisoned patient is hard to be predicted—many a time, or rather, quite often, it happens that the patient responding to the treatment goes suddenly worse and then to death. Actually, the heavy blows of the wash-outs of the stomach go beyond their tolerance." He described like a doctor would do.

Here Animesh happened to remember a Bhoju of his turf many years ago who'd also taken poison. He'd responded to the treatment well enough—say, speaking, eating little by little, but died a few days later leaving everybody in wonder.

"You can't tell until three or four days go by," Maity said. "I'm trying to help you the hardest. I'll catch the best *logna,* that is, the best moments of the full moon tomorrow for the grand Vedic Sacrifices on fire at Nimatala Grand Crematoriums. ('Logna' is a special short period of time most appropriate for any ritual work). By the time you'll be chanting Lord Shiva Mantras. I'll give it to you now," he said and turned towards the place of the Goddess. He took a yellow piece of paper out of the small diary and held it to him. It was already written on it. "Here you are," he said. Animesh took it in his hand and unfolded it. It had Sanskrit words in Bengali letters in red ink: *Om Namaha Shivaya.*

"Chant this mantra as many times as you can, anytime, anywhere, at leisure or at work. The more chants, the better results," he suggested.

"Can I chant it in the back of my mind; I mean silently?" Animesh asked.

"Yes, you can." Animesh put it carefully in a brown envelope in his bag pocket and thanked him.

"When's your bus?" Maity asked as he gave him ambrosia from the plate in front of Goddess. He took it in his right hand palm with his left hand touching under the right palm and leant his head down in deep respect for Goddess Kali. "There are many buses at a fifteen-minute interval up to Katwa, but the only bus that goes near my home is at 5:15," Animesh answered hesitantly. "But I think I'll go around Bandel-way with you by way of Nabadwip." He put the sweet ball of ambrosia into his mouth.

Maity looked a bit confused. "Won't it be a long way around and time consuming?"

While eating the sweet ball he replied, "About double of the time if I went straight down the bus route," and paused shortly, "all the same I'd like it."

It wasn't hard for Maity to realize that he was too scared to travel straightway; the longer he could stay with him, the safer he'd feel.

"Okay then," Maity said smiling. "Let's get the 4:15 train," he suggested.

"I'm ready," Animesh said looking down at himself indicating with his hands that he was already dressed up. Animesh had the idea etched in his mind that Maity'd told him the previous day that they might have sued against him to the police who might be looking for him. He also remembered him telling on that night of the cursed phone call that all the laws about the women cases were in favour of them. Whatever way they would report against a man, he would be in great trouble. Just as reporters would rush over with a smell of a piece of spicy news, so would the cops to start a case or squeeze money out of the victim, without waiting to confirm if the so-called accused was guilty or not.

The journey on the EMU train to Bandel was not like other days' journey to Barrackpore on Amway business when he'd mostly read a book or looked out of the window at the open field. Today's journey was boring and sad and tremulous. Sitting by the window next to Maity, talking to him less, but listening to him more, and chanting Lord Shiva Mantra in between, in the back of his mind, he was heading for Bandel. Maity told him a lot about his performance on tantra-work. He listened to it trustfully that his tantras would tide him over this time.

When the train was about to get in at Bandel Junction, everybody got to know from the extra acute noise of passing across a number of tracks to its specified track to the platform. People to get off at Bandel started standing up from their seats, reaching down their bags from the racks above or taking them out from under the seats.

"So, you're gonna get off here," Maity said knowingly. "Anyway, don't worry yourself sick. Don't let anxiety get you. Everything will be okay, soon in three or four days' time." He said in consolation sliding his hand down his back.

"This four-day period is the thing to think about. This is the period that is most dangerous. It can topple everything of our expectation. Who knows where I'll be and how—during this period. You can speak light of it but the one who is caught in the fire, knows what it is like," he thought heaving a sigh of hopelessness.

"Do the things as I asked you to, use your free time and keep your faith. Keep in touch with me," he advised. "Stay lucky." He raised his hand up in a blessing mode.

Animesh got up and stood behind the people already lined up to get off. The train screeched to a halt, they pushed forward to get off through the clamour. He stepped over to the window and Maity waved him goodbye. He stood there until the train started off.

He looked for a place to sit down but there wasn't any. So, he wandered about the platform lazily and thoughtfully having knocks and pushes from the people moving about.

Chapter 38

The local train for Katwa Junction came eight minutes late. He got scared to see the train unusually crowded. He got on the train the hard way but couldn't get inside from the doors. It was damn hard to find enough space to land your feet on the train floor. It was crowded mostly with the Nabadwip and Mayapur-ISKCON visitors and also with Shri Shukdeva Brahmhachariya's disciples to Dainhat Sukdeva's ashram. Many male disciples of Shukdev's wore a vest and dhoti, or trousers, with a thin towel tied around their waists. They were beating big flat drums and maracas and *kasor, (i.e. a thick brass dish making high banging sounds),* along with it went over the passengers' clamour. Animesh regretted extremely that he'd clean forgotten about this day that before the Holi Festival day, the Up-trains would be over crowded with Sukdeva's devotees like the previous years. Nearly a quarter of a million people would visit his ashram in three days.

Shri Sukhdeva was a great famous Hindu saint who passed away years ago, to whose *Samadhi* Services Animesh had gone with Ranajit to offer a fistful of earth in the *Samadhi* pit. One day at his ripe old age, Shri Sukdeva had said to his disciples present there, "Now that you people of science travel in space or go to the moon unimaginably hard way, spending billions of bucks, taking so long time, risking your lives so greatly, but I go there any time I like to—if I go in the morning, I get back in the evening." People didn't take it that serious because it sounded absurd to them. They wouldn't know the power of Yoga. No-one would know of it unless they get into that grade of yoga and meditation.

Animesh knew there would be no hope for a seat till Nabadwip came and after Nabadwip there was only thirty-five minutes' journey left till his station came. With his hard efforts he was able to inch up to the middle space from the doors and stood there helplessly.

The thought of foreboding about the girl in hospital bobbed up in his mind too often. When passengers were chatting, calling one another, pushing about, jostling about, and disciples were beating their drums in a slow rhythm in high-decibel sound in joy; the train hawkers shouting their slogans nudging their way through the crowd stubbornly like pig-ignorant creatures, Animesh kept standing helplessly in that crazy crowd with his hard-packed bag hanging from his shoulder, his hands gripping two handles above his head, and chanting *'Om Namaha Shivaya'*. Tremor was smashing through him. He headed for home, sometimes chanting the mantra and sometimes having the pinches of the foreboding through his heart. His face said he was the saddest person on the train.

Around eight o' clock in the evening, he got in home. Even being back at home he couldn't feel easy enough, because here too, he thought, if the news broke out in the papers, people of his town would come to know of it all and cops might be on the lookout for him. He had no place to live safely for then. To stay in peace to some extent he wanted to stay at somebody else's home away from his village but he couldn't do that because he'd have to let them know the reasons behind it.

Afraid in hell, he didn't go out on a cruise as usual to meet his friends or wanted anybody to meet him until the crisis was over. He decided to spend the evening in silence keeping himself from facing up with his family members for fear of being caught in their doubts. The sounds of beating the drums of the disciples walking to Sukhdeva's Ashram came into his ears from the main road. He only kept himself pent up in worries and concern chanting the Shiva Mantra.

Chapter 39

Yesterday he called Maity in the evening after he'd arrived at home. Today was the full moon. From the morning there was a rejoicing noise from kids playing colours with one another, chasing one another to colour them on the road. Those were the days for him too; they were far away now. For many years he only watched them coloring one another. But today Animesh didn't even get out to the yard to watch them play coloring like the other years. Only that he sometimes peeked at the road through the balcony grill, or lay on the bed or sitting in the chair dejectedly and chanting the Shiva Mantra in between. From time to time he thought what the hell happened to him!

He bathed early on the tube well nook, got back into his room, left the door closed on the bolt and sat cross-legged on the bare red floor with the wet towel wrapped around his waist and started chanting the Shiva Mantra *"Om Namaha Shivaya."* Quite some time later, Sumitra, his mother called into the room and turned the handle which was locked. He jumped to his feet and left the wet towel off his waist and put on his loongie quickly so as not to let her doubt. She thought he'd locked the door not to let anyone in to colour him. She came in to take out the soiled clothes for washing.

The whole day rolled to be the afternoon. The sun tilted. But he couldn't communicate with Maity. His anxiety increased. Night came down and grew older but still he couldn't get him on the phone. It sounded switched off. "What is it? Why's the phone still off?" He thought irately. He felt weak from the long-running shivers. He didn't mean to have a supper but it would raise questions and doubts, so he ate a little.

He tried to call Maity for the last time before he hit the sack. No dice. It thrust him into deeper concern. He lay in bed till late and then fell into a light sleep with his restive brain—

The police were outside his house asking around people on the road when he was eating lunch. Oh hell, Oh God! It's the cops!" He drew in his breath. He couldn't finish eating. He'd have to rush; flee away. He found himself running down the opposite side and by the side and the slope of the ponds, down the dusty narrow road towards the railway line, the cops following him far behind. He ran across the railway line, farther away planning to catch the bus to any directions from the High Road. He ran and ran puffing more and more. He couldn't move faster as before. He could hear the jeep horn behind him getting closer and closer. His leg were brushing and knocking against the other. Suddenly he fell down bang on the dusty country-road full of pits. He was now falling down the hill into a trench.

His original sounds came out loud and he woke up. "Cops!" He felt his original legs heavy as if hard to move from fear. His body sweated lightly. He lay stiff from fear as if real cops were waiting for him outside. "It was a bad dream, luckily!" He thought. He thanked God it was not real. A deep sigh went out through his nose. He thought of calling Arijit Maity right away but the clock on the wall said four-twenty; still a long time to go before he'd leave the bed. He lay quiet thinking of all evils with his heart throbbing beneath. "Does the nightmare mean it is going to be true?" he asked himself many times.

Chapter 40

Since morning he crazily tried to call Maity, but still failed. He couldn't learn the latest about the girl in life-and-death risk in hospital, nor was he able to learn about the aimed Vedic Sacrifice on Fire. His tremulous heart became heavier; his face looked blue and dry and shrunk. He felt unbalanced in standing from the shivers inside. The nightmare chased him into a deep concern and gradually into a panic—the panic of cops. He chanted the Mantra more and more.

Half the day he spent in breathtaking situation. After his bath at twelve as usual, he was chanting the Shiva Mantra the same way; half way through, the mobile trilled on the bed. He stopped chanting and jumped to his feet and looked down at the mobile screen. It was Arijit Maity, at last. Pressing down the green button quickly he said, "Hello, I've been trying to get you since yesterday morning." His voice sounded terror-stricken. "You can't imagine how I have spent the time since then."

"I was worried about you too," Maity's suppressed voice came. "I had no chance to keep it on. I did three Vedic Services on Fire and the worshipping in your name. I'll tell you," he said. "I came to Burdwan late this morning again."

"Why? What's new?" Animesh asked.

"Something big," Maity said. It shook Animesh's heart again. Another ominous thought hit him. "Did the girl die then?" he asked himself. "What's the matter? Please tell me."

"In the room under your cot in the right hand corner there was a poisonous snake of medium size, curled up."

"Snake!" he sucked in sharply. "Under my cot!?"

"Yes, snake." He repeated. "Their sangoma hexed it onto you."

"What more do they still have to do?" Animesh asked angrily. Maity could hear him panting into the phone.

"The snake's been caught and I thought of keeping it for you to see it but it would've been too risky to keep it 'cos it was under a spell."

"What did you see in the sacrificial meditation?" He asked.

"The situation is still grave. It's a war with them. The sangoma's been working his hardest to succeed. It might even turn worse."

"Still worse?" Animesh asked fearfully and became speechless for a moment. He wouldn't be reassured until there is a sign of the girl getting better. "Cops might be looking for you. They seemed to be using cops as well with political influence. Try to keep off as much as possible." He warned him once again. Here the last night's dream hit him.

"What do you mean?" Animesh asked nervously. "Does it mean she died?"

"Might have, however, it's not possible to see things like you see them in the mirror. Till yesterday night she worsened farther."

"Oh my God!" He exclaimed. How much more do I have to go through?" One of his hands flew up to his temple in extreme hopelessness. "What ever should I do now ! My brains aren't working. It'll drive me nuts."

"Be firm, have faith in God. It'll blow over." He provided guts for him. "If you can, come back to Burdwan," he advised him. Animesh thought for a moment. The mobile still held on his ear. Let me see to it." He cut off the call.

Animesh thought, "If the cops went to my school, they would get my home address and photos from the office." He felt his blood getting chilled through his veins. He wanted to stay in hiding at somebody else's. He had places to stay, but he'd have to face a number of questions, and it'd make things come to light beforehand; it wasn't possible. After a lot of wild thinking, he decided to go back to Burdwan at last. He deeply thought of what might happen, if at all: "The police, if turned up here, will be searching for any documents like letters from that girl or photos of her for proofs, and they will certainly be rummaging through my files, scattering things around into a jumble. But, if anything ruining should happen to me, let it happen out there in Burdwan, it might be limited to the unknown place whereas it'd spread out like wild fire hereabouts."

His mother tried to open the door. It didn't open. "Is it locked?" she asked.

He opened the door and she got in to give him ambrosia of Lord Krishna from the next-door neighbour. He took the bowl from her hand. "One thing, mum," he said, "I'll go back to Burdwan right today."

"Right today?" she asked. "Can't it keep for the day?" She knew the next day was a holiday, too.

"It's urgent," he replied.

"Then I will fix your lunch soon. Let me see how far she is with her cooking." She went across the yard into the kitchen where his brother's wife was cooking.

About a quarter to three he started out on his bicycle with the black duffel-bag packed up with washed clothes. He didn't dare go down the straightaway route to Katwa. Instead he rode across the main road at Mihijampara bus stop and down the way across the lowland and along the levee of the river Bhagirathi, rattling on the uneven earthen road parallel with the main road half a kilometer apart, then across the main road again at Panuhat Bazar and through the alleyway, then again down the wide main street towards the bus terminus.

Just before the railway gate, his weary eyes fell on three cops coming up on foot. His heart shook in sudden fear and doubt. "Do they have any case on me? Have they already been out to get me?" He thought frighteningly. "Did they have any information from the school? They must have a photo of me then!" He figured out many things as the cops were coming up. He stole a quick look out of the corners of his eyes trying to see if they were observing him. He turned his face away praying to God to spare him. The cops passed by him without looking at him. He found his life back again. He thanked God. So long as he was on the bus all the way up to Burdwan, he sat cringed from deep concern and not wanting to be observed by anybody, chanting the Shiva Mantra and wondering how another three days would pass away. Whoever or whatever is born it dies. This trouble too, must end but how it will end was the thing that was killing him.

Chapter 41

During those horrendous days that he had been in horrible terror, he had a lesson that women could trap anybody anytime anywhere and harm them ruthlessly to spoil their life. From then he thought women were dormant dangers and thus were distrustful. He even shook off the idea of getting married forever. Those black days were over and without any personal harm to him or being bothered anyway, except for a good amount of money for Vedic Sacrifices. He began to pass the days wearily; not thinking of or looking at women.

Anyway those days went away far enough. Half a year later, Anamika began to creep back in his love-torn heart. Again the thought of her in his loneliness stirred him. Again he imagined her, the days in college, at the time he'd practised singing in the choir for Teachers' Day, and sang on the annual function in marvelous adornment and so on.

Actually women are such a peculiar type of living beings on the beautiful earth that without them men can't get by, and without men women are not worth. Without women the world is dead—the earth is like a garden without flowers. Just as natural things are the beauty of the earth, so are the women the beauty of the civilization. Men work hard and climb up in a good social position because they want a beautiful woman for their combination. Men even fought and lost their lives and kingdoms in wars to obtain beautiful women in the past. So, it was not too wrong that Anamika started coming back instinctively to his thoughts at leisure. And yet misfortune didn't quit him. Anamika's news came to him in waves but it didn't glue up his broken heart, or rather it broke his ribs over his heart one after another.

It was another formal visit of Animesh to Arnab in the evening in his same old rented room. After the preliminaries were over, Arnab said, "I've got a piece of good news to give you, friend." He smiled while straining the tea into the cups for themselves standing over the gas oven. Animesh was sitting on the stool diagonally behind him. "However, I wonder how good it will be for you," he added.

Animesh naturally being very attentive looked up at his face.

"What's the good news, Arnab that you've been carrying for me?" Animesh asked curiously. "Just a moment," Arnab said and handed him a cup and took another for himself and seated himself on another stool in front of him. "Move over to the bedstead," he said pulling the stool to his bed, Animesh followed suit. They placed the cups and saucers on the bed and sat on the stools next to it. Animesh tried to guess what sort of good news it could be.

"Oh, I forgot the cookies. Wait, I'll get them," he said and was about to get them. "No cookies. Only tea is better." Animesh held him back and took a sip from his cup because he was impatient for the news. "Tell me the 'good news' instead." He looked at his face eagerly.

"The news is," he took the first sip at his cup, "Anamika's been appointed at a high school," Arnab said smiling after he had another sip at his cup.

"Has she?" Animesh reacted enthusiastically. "It's a very good piece of news," Animesh said and smiled. "Where did she join?" he asked.

"I don't know exactly where," Arnab answered. "Down in the countryside." He gestured to the east. "About two hour's bus journey."

"She can commute from home," Animesh added but the next moment he realized the reality behind it was that it'd carry her farther and farther away and beyond his reach. She'd already had a Master's and now a teacher, while Animesh was a graduate. His face turned blue with concern but he suppressed it and said, "A very good student like her deserved to get it, and she did. If she is determined to get further up, she will be able to. She's had class."

Love was like hypnosis. You can't escape from it so easily. For the past few days he thought of her a lot. He thought if she'd been coincidently posted to a school in his home town, there would have been a point for him to get further up. Heavenly God could have done at least this much for him. But what he couldn't realize was what wasn't to happen would never happen, no matter how hard you tried or dreamed of; you're on the roll of the rules.

Chapter 42

Six months dragged by through the good and the bad. July was on its second week. It had been raining all day that had started in the previous afternoon. Arijit Maity asked, "Do you have to go to school today? Isn't it a rainy day for school?"

"It might be a rainy day. It depends on what percent of students turn up," Animesh answered. "What else can I do here? Besides, who knows if the rain lets off after ten o'clock? My casual leave will be gone for no reason."

When he got out, the rain let up to a drizzle. The sky was grey-black and heavy, a light wind was on. Bus Terminus was half as crowded as compared to the other days. Suddenly, he stopped short. To his surprise, Anamika's sloe eyes met Animesh's small ones, and her lips stretched into a sudden chuckle, and then asked, "How are you?" and he made the proper reply the same way nodding his head to her "I'm fine", she as quickly looked down; mindful of her steps on the oozy surface as she walked cautiously towards her bus, one of her hands holding her sari and the other gripping the umbrella over her head. He didn't have chance to ask her how she was. She, however, didn't stop or slow down but Animesh held to that spot instinctively. So unexpected it was that he couldn't believe his eyes. His gaze fell on her back until she walked up and stepped into her bus some fifteen meters away. He folded his umbrella and stepped into his bus near him and sat by the window of the almost empty bus. He looked out through the window trying to meet her eyes once again or at least to see her in the bus. But probably she'd sat down and was out of sight. The more the time passed, the more he reminisced about the scene sadly— "Why didn't I speak to her right away or call after her and go over to speak to her in courtesy. I could have got off the bus and found out her or I could have travelled along on her bus some distance and talked to her. I could have spoken to her and known her mind at the least. She didn't shook me off completely. What harm would it have done to me if I hadn't gone to school on such a rainy day? Such an opportunity wouldn't come even once in a blue moon."

Another blunder, another failure—the prick of this regret pierced him for many days, a series of failures. How many times more would God give him chances? He cursed himself 'worthless'. We hope and live and, we live and hope. "Will there be another moment like this, to see her at the least?" He thought vaguely.

Chapter 43

Agrahayan of Bengali calendar falls in November and December. It's often dubbed as the month of marriage. It was said to be the ideal time for getting a wife home.

Abhirup Adhikary invited the whole staff at his wedding reception. It fell two days after the marriage date as usual. The school was let off at the recess for them to attend his reception at his country house in Hoogly district near the southern border of Burdwan district.

A red-white minibus was waiting at the bifurcation at Shamsunder Bazar for invitees to come over. Ramesh, Mrinmoy, Nabarun, Arun. Kopil, Animesh, already came. Sometime later Paran and Prasant turned up, followed by Sumonto—the newly appointed clerk, and Sabir and Kamal. And then came Korrim Khan, the most popular teacher in the school for his comedies. Animesh was a bit more excited than the others because Anamika was also an invitee at his reception. It was a chance for him to absorb her in his eyes and have a talk if possible but he kept it in himself.

He looked at his watch. It was near half past six. The night had already come down but many of the attendees didn't arrive yet. Although, it was said that the bus would start at half past six, a quarter to seven at the latest but there was no sign of the start.

By half past seven, most of them arrived and most of them were sitting in the bus and others were around.

Time was being wasted. By eight o'clock only one woman para-teacher was yet to turn up. She was called several times; each time the answer came she'd soon be up. Everybody was so annoyed at her being unusually, insensitively late. Animesh looked at his watch pointedly several times and clucked his tongue. "Why should she ever go with the people of punctuality? Why won't she go individually?" he said angrily into the noise of their talk.

"Where there are women, there is some trouble with the work," Korrim commented sarcastically from deep annoyance while waiting with a few teachers near the door of the bus.

"Don't badmouth of us women, Korrim-babu," Ahona protested. "Not all women are the same. Do you know when I came here? You couldn't turn up before me." Her voice was serious.

"Won't you let her adorn herself to her heart's content? She is going to attend a wedding ceremony in the crowd of so many people," Kamal said out with a sarky tone.

"She wants a good half of the day to adorn herself, then why should she bother us with her adornment at the journey-time?" Animesh said angrily.

"What's the good of getting spruced up spending a lot of costly cosmetics and so much time if she arrives there in the empty place around midnight? Isn't it crazy," Korrim said.

"That's it," Sabir said with a short laugh in a thin voice. "What if all the viewers go away?"

When the most-late woman rolled up, some guys yelled enthusiastically, "There she comes." It was like some queen came to honour them with a kind visit. Some of them stared at her pointedly in a way that they were rather annoyed. She, however, felt no compunction. She got on the bus and sat in a nice reserved seat.

The bus started with a chug. It was a quarter to eight. "Shit!" said Animesh, "When the heck will they reach, who knows? On the way ahead Rasbihari, Pratik, and Protap would be picked up. Animesh thought, "If they got back home from the bus-stop, it'd take time again. They had called us several times in the meantime."

"Driver, we're late right, but still no need to run too fast in the night," Korrim warned. When the commotion calmed down, Mrinmoy said, "Korrim-sahib, tell us a joke."

Korrim said two standing jokes but they didn't go over. So, he was down after Ramesh. He often made fun of him because Ramesh was the calmest guy in the school. He was short-height, dark skinned, amicable man with a sweet round face. Everybody loved him.

The bus came to a stop finally. Animesh looked down at his watch again. A quarter to nine; they got off the vehicle and looked over at the light and the temporarily made entrance gate. The house was a bit inside. The lights indicated the way in. They walked slowly. A little way up turning to the left was the cloth pandal adorned with lights. The dull noise from the two power generators began to annoy the ears along with the fast music, and also the smoke of the generators trickled the nose. Abhirup was not around. A boy was sent down to message him of their presence. Soon enough he came smiling, "Welcome, welcome, very warm welcome, sir and madams," he said as he was approaching, his hand stretching out for Korrim's hand, followed by Protap, Rashbihari, and Pratik's, who were in front of him. "Madam, very nice you've come." He nodded to Ahona. "Mita ma'am didn't come?" he asked.

"No, she didn't. She didn't have the okay from her authority," Ahona answered jokingly. "Abhirup, you look like a prince today," Protap said admiringly. Others smiled in agreement saying, "Certainly." Animesh's eyes were secretly on the lookout for the one he was pulled by.

Abhirup smiled broadly to hear the broad compliment. He wore golden sherwani with fine work done almost all over, the red thin scarf hung from his neck down his front. The gold chain hung down his chest.

"What made you late?" He asked with a touch of complaint. "Getting all of us together got us late," Korrim said keeping the real reason dark. Animesh's mind was whirling to see Anamikia. He couldn't help asking about her. He went and stood beside Abhirup. "Didn't she come?" he asked softly.

Abhirup turned his head to him. "Yes, she did come. She just left probably when you got in," he answered. "She'd come early enough."

"She came n' went out for home as well!" he exclaimed in despondency. "What a bad luck!" he exclaimed again; "If I could have come a little more early! Shit!" He would have had a chance to speak to her at least and seen her with his heart. The scene of that rainy day of her speaking to him in a free mind at the bus-terminus floated before his eyes. He still hoped she'd change her mind to his favour. It was a chance to talk to her. His felt warm in anger. His blood was climbing up his head. "It was only because of that woman, everything is bungled; she made a real balls-up." He said under his breath gnashing his teeth that nobody heard or saw.

Paran Kumar Khan was impatient. "Let's give the present to the bride, first," he said. "We have to go back a long way again." So, they went over to the bride's place. Abhirup introduced his colleagues to his wife in bulk and reeled out the names of them to her. She must have been confused.

"Take care of my friend," Protap Sarker said looking at the bride, both of his hands around Abhirup. "He's a very good boy. We hereby hand him over to you," he said funnily with a smile when others too smiled with him. She blushed a little and chuckled in answer. "You don't have to introduce Abhi to her," Rasbihari said emphatically. "They've already known each other better to take care of themselves." Sabir, Mrinmoy, and Protap laughed loudly.

"That's true. It's a plus point to know a girl beforehand," Protap said mockingly. "So, I got the licking. I never knew mine beforehand."

"Do you have any trouble in knowing her afterwards?" Rashbihari asked Protap.

Paran K. Khan lowered his head towards Animesh. "Why are they getting late? Don't they know the night is getting older? It's a winter night." Sunk-heart Animesh didn't want to be late at all for his objective failed.

Some guys around heard Paran's reasonable words and said, "Yes, we should go and eat now. It's nine thirty."

The dinner pandal was separated from the main one. The soft music of Tagore's songs by V. Balsara on the instrument made a very special ambience for the invitees here. In the middle of eating, Korrim cracked a self-made joke out of the eating situation. One of the catering boys came checking if anybody wanted more fried rice. He offered Korrim leaning down forward and holding a pot of fried rice on one hand and a scoop in the other, ready to give rice.

"Can I give you some more rice?" He asked.

"Then, does it cost me any extra for the extra rice?" Korrim asked seriously casting a brief look at the boy. Mrinmoy, Sabir opposite him, and Arun next to him burst into a loud laughter, almost being chocked. They caught the fun. But the caterer boy got puzzled at this and looked down at them in wonder. In fact, in a sidewalk hotel they would charge extra for extra rice. Kopil and Protap from the table behind asked, "What did Korrim-babu say?" They looked over at their table stopping eating for a moment.

"Give him, give him," Sabir told the catering boy pointing with his finger, still laughing. The boy gave him one full scoop of fried rice and was about to give another but he held his hand spread over his plate. "No, no, not anymore," he said emphatically, "I have only one small bag. The rest of the emptiness is for the finishing items."

They laughed again shortly. In fact, when somebody is known to be a joke maker, whatever he speaks, people find it funny. Animesh with Paran at the next table called, "What's up? Roll of laughter while eating?"

"Korrim sir made a nice joke". Mrinmoy called and laughed again.

Rasbihari said, "Korrim-sahib is Korrim-sahib, always, and everywhere." Prasant khan and Pratik Chattoraj were behind Animesh. "But we missed such a nice joke, you mean?" Pratik asked jokingly. "Tell us once again," he demanded. Korrim said smiling, "I was talking about rice offers."

"It won't come out that good now. Everything has its ripening time. When it comes naturally, it provides its best quality," said Mrinmoy. Anyway, Animesh came back home broken hearted.

Chapter 44

The first week of February 2007, Maity broke the news over tea about himself. Animesh himself brought the evening tea today. They were drinking it sitting on the bed. It was about half past seven. "Today I'm going to give you a piece of good news," He announced and looked up at Animesh's face to read it. "Guess what?"

"Good news! He says!" Animesh couldn't make a guess, he took another sip at his earthen cup and held it in his hand. "What's the good news?" he asked back.

"Try to guess," Maity insisted. Animesh looked past him and thought, his teacup still held in his hand. He brought his look back to Maity. "I don't have any idea." He surrendered and took another sip at his cup.

Maity sipped twice quickly and poured some more tea into his cup from the rest left in the steel glass and proffered the glass to Animesh. He held out his cup ahead and he poured out all into his cup that came to the full.

"So, you couldn't tell, eh?" Maity asked smiling.

"No, not any idea," he admitted.

"I'm going to be transferred."

"Transferred?" Animesh asked in disbelief.

"Yes. I think I had told you before your horrible days." He tried to remind him.

Animesh's face changed a little, "So you're getting transferred," he mumbled. Maity observed it.

"Where are you getting transferred?" Animesh asked.

"To Barasat," he answered. "They could have sent you to Calcutta," Animesh said unsatisfactorily. "It would have been your home city."

"They won't do it right now. I had been there many years," he said. Barasat was the district head quarters of North 24 Parganas, a part of Calcutta.

They put down the cups in the plastic net basket under Maity's bed. Won't you miss me?" He asked.

"Yes, I will." He looked up at his face. "And you?"

"Yes, I'll miss you out very much. You'll be in my heart," Maity said. Animesh knew they were the conning words; out of sight, out of mind.

"Keep in touch with me," Arijit Maity said.

"I will, of course. I will need you." Animesh said.

"So, when do you have to join the new office?" He asked looking up at his face.

"Soon enough; as soon as I've straightened things out here," said Maity.

"All the same?" he wanted to know an approximate time.

"In less than a week." Maity answered.

"Quite soon," Animesh said sort of despondently. "I'll be lonely then."

"Yes, you'll be lonely, I know. But it's a job. I would have to move out today or tomorrow." He paused a little. "You'll get a room partner soon," he reassured.

"Who knows what sort of a man he will be?" Animesh tossed his hands.

"Whoever comes, all you have to do is adjust with him. He'll eat his, live his way, and you'll eat yours and live your own way. You'll have no problem. You keep yourself in studies. Let him screw up with himself. Nobody has to bother." Maity suggested with explanations.

"I'll see to it," Animesh said softly. "And still if I find him annoying and not adjustable at all, I'll find a new place. I might even go to over to Shyamsunder. I'll be closer to my school and save my time."

""That place I should object to," he said quickly with a tone of protest. "Try not to be living near your school."

Animesh remembered the sore of those black horrible days and shook his head. In fact, the thought about Anamika being back pushed the memory of the horrible days behind.

"I'm sorry. I know how dangerous it could be out there but I'd forgotten of that place. I'll never ever stay near my school," he said in correction.

"Better try so you can get transferred from that area," he advised.

"I've been trying my best but the worthless communist government has just deceived me over and over again. I already reached three times at the viva board of the SSC, but the government has made up its mind that they will no way let me go out of this place. If not, how in hell could they push me so far away to a school at the border of Bihar at the second time's appointment when the ministry had already announced that the teachers at faraway schools would be posted near in their next appointment?" Animesh recalled it once again.

"Be cool," he said. "Bad luck has always chased you every way you took. That's why I gave you the protection." Maity took a short pause. "Keep faith on your own ability. God on high will look up at you today or tomorrow." The words of consolation and sympathy at least left some hope in him.

"I'll still be appearing at the exam until I'm tired of it or unless the authority prevents me from taking exams."

In less than a week the day came. Maity was leaving Burdwan today. He had already carried most of the things, especially the sample medicines and other heavy loads.

Animesh had a bath earlier than usual. He dressed up and sat down on the edge of the bed and looked up at Maity, who stopped checking on his register, and looked at Animesh. "Feeling bad, eh?" He asked.

"Yes, a bit, of course." Animesh replied.

"So, do I." Maity said, "At least two years together, sharing many things of our lives." He paused shortly, "Anyway, all will be alright. Don't think too much of them."

"I don't want to, but thinking wouldn't wait for one's persuasion. It just pushes its way brazenly and stubbornly."

"So, it should, but you too have to be stubborn and brazen to it," Maity suggested.

Animesh said nothing to it. He looked down at his watch and slowly stood up.

Maity gave him a hug and patted on his back saying, "God be with you." He looked at his watch. There was still a little time in hand for his bus. "Sit down a while," he urged.

Suddenly his voice changed into graveness. "Now listen to me good, brother," Maity said. "Don't take it otherwise." He paused. "Find out a good beautiful lady and marry her and be settled." Animesh found this advice was in line with his own folks. So, he wasn't easy with listening to it. "Don't wait for Anamika. What I got to know is that she'll never ever change her arrogant high ambitious mind. She's now even higher in qualification and job position, too. This is the bare truth. She floats on the air. You shouldn't be silly trying to rush behind her." Animesh listened to him with no reaction, though he found it true. Maity continued, "If she had come to your life at all, you wouldn't have kept her under your control. Rather, she'd have dominated you rather ruthlessly because you're a soft simple-minded guy. And because of your blind, overflowing love for her, you wouldn't have known that she was twirling you around her finger. And your life would have turned into a dammed hell in no time."

"I will remember this, dada," Animesh said coldly.

"Tell me if I have to go visiting a bride with you. I'll go," he reassured.

Animesh stood up with his bag, Maity, too, stood up and stroked his hair affectionately. They exchanged their looks for the last time.

Chapter 45

Animesh felt rather lonely after Maity had left. He mostly spent his leisure time like he had in the individual room—reading, listening to music on the cheap cassette player, or listening to the BBC and Voice of America because now there was none to feel irritated, or object to his listening. He spent his time his own way for a month. Then he heard that someone would come to the empty seat. So, he thought of moving out to a rented room what he'd planned when he came back here after his B. Ed. course but he couldn't; he was tied to the place because of Arijit Maity.

Prakash Chakraborty found him a rental and took him to talk about it with its owner a little inside from the Curzon Gate Cross Roads area. After they had rung the doorbell, they were let in by a woman who seemed to be the maid of the house. They stood on the small wall-enclosed yard of the two-storied building, good enough. An old man in a white dhoti and a white fine panjabi shirt came out and stood in the door way of the veranda in front of them. It was around half past five in the evening. On his skinny tall body his hair was thin and all white; his face was shaved with no moustache. At a glance anybody would respect him for his real gentleman-like appearance.

"Uncle, this teacher wants to rent a room," Prakash said looking up at him standing on the yard, Animesh next to him.

The old man eyed Animesh from head down to his feet. "What's your name?" he asked.

"Ahindra Bhabook."

"Ahindra what?" he asked again.

"Bhabook—means a thinker."

"So you are a thinker. "Mr. Thinker, do you think you will rent my house?" He asked with the initial irony. "There are two rooms together with attached bathroom, and all prvilleges?" He pointed ahead to his right, "All time water."

"First let me see it." Animesh demanded.

"I'll show you, of course," said the man. "What do you do?" He asked.

"He's a teacher," Prakash answered before Animesh did.

"Primary?" he asked disdainfully.

"No. At a high school," Animesh replied.

"Oh, I see," he said twisting his lips into a bitter irony and eyed him up and down once again. Animesh's temper had already begun to fray. He already knew he wasn't getting into that 'hell'.

"How much do you get paid that you can pay the rent for my house?" He charged. He stared down at him all the time. Now he looked down at Prakash.

"Prakash, who have you brought over?" He charged him now. His eyes didn't look any better than a devil's. "Don't you know how precious time is?" He asked accusingly. And right away he corrected himself. "Oh, you wouldn't know the value of time." Prakash also felt insulted at his rough behaviour. His face shrunk. Animesh's blood was up. He couldn't ever imagine how such an old man looking like a real gentleman could ever insult anybody at his door so nastily who came to him as a client. He stared at the nose of the old shit and felt like giving it a hard punch to bleed like a river.

"Prakash, where have you brought me over?" Animesh asked intending for the old man to hear him and blaze his core. "Is this a place to live in? I'm no' gonna take it even if it comes free of cost. Just by walking on two feet, a creature can't be a human. It takes the real quality for a human." He snapped. "I see he's got on the hill of arrogance with s-o-m-e money." He pronounced 'some' lengthily and continued. "There are millions of people on the earth with a million times more money than this guy. They wouldn't hold this much arrogance. Come along," he told Prakash pulling at his hand lightly and they both stamped out of that hell.

"What did you say? I-I am, ..." he started stammering. They walked out and stopped at the entrance.

"I said I was in the wrong so long to think that all living beings walking on two feet were humans. But now I knew I carried the wrong idea," Animesh said loudly turning around towards the old man. "You'd better walk on four feet." They heard the old man stammering protests like crazy as they stamped out of the boundary door.

"He's an insane shit," Prakash said walking.

"Insane or sick, or whatever," Animesh said, "When he's caught in the right grip, he'd fuck his own ass and would know what it costs to make people small. People wouldn't have patience to diagnose any disease in his head."

Animesh quit the idea of living in a rental. It would be costly. Besides, he would have to have somebody cook for him. So, he decided to find the mess house that Arnab had told him about a year before.

In the third week of May he got to know that there was a seat still unoccupied in Swallow Nest. He decided to get in there.

Chapter 46

Animesh'd taken about twelve years before he decided to try all out for a plumb job as an assistant teacher because he'd risked losing the time in crazy attempts at getting out to a developed foreign country to work and live. It died the death. Now it was another twelve years (about) since he joined Golapnagar Greenfield General Intermediate & High School. In total 24 years of the most precious golden period of his rarest human life went down the drain. What could a person do after that?

Looking at him for once, you could discover him differently. White threads of beard appeared in great numbers. The man of a decade back who would shave thrice a week wouldn't shave more than once a week now. He felt too bored to prune the white threads of his moustache. Streaks of white hair also appeared above his forehead. The man who used to sing into the air or croon to himself with pleasure or no pleasure didn't even feel like listening to music much. His face changed; his eyes got in, and brown crinkles came evident under his eyes. His thought changed, too. He wouldn't get fired easily, wouldn't get into argument over a trifle as before. He mostly kept himself to himself. In the past few years he had been truthfully careless about himself. He became like an oar-broken boat let loose down the stream and flowed away with no particular destination. The time-honoured colourful earth looked faded to him, seeming all the colours mixed into a blurred grey color. Only the red of a rainbow when appeared in the sky would come to his notice and warn him about anything he thought of. He wryly thought that his most precious human life was wasted. What he knew was he'd have to run the life and drag the body as long as his soul lived in him.

He spent six years in the Swallow Nest. He was bored of living in Swallow Nest anymore; it was a famous old mess house on the Banka River. Shibam Mahato, Binomro Bhaat, Probhash Gangopaddhay, Asutosh Mondal had been transferred. Anup had gone back to his village school by a mutual transfer. Umanath, the cook had gone home in Ghatshila for two months. The new young men took their places. The ambience of this mess changed for the worse and worse. They were undisciplined. They drank every evening and hollered and played rock in high pitch which was unbearable to him. He couldn't concentrate his mind in reading or living in there peacefully. The new irregular cook was another pigheaded man. He bunked off his work quite often. His cooking was not palatable to him either. In all truth, it became all impossible to live in Swallow Nest.

Hemlal Kisku asked him, "Master, there goes a whisper that you're leaving the mess house, next month?" Teachers were often dubbed as 'master'.

"Yes," Animesh replied in brief. "At last. It's time for me to." He looked at his face eagerly asking. "But who told you this great secret?" Hemlal was one of the old boarders, skinny health, dark-skinned middle-age man now, working at a panchayat office beyond Burdwan town.

"A little bird told me." Hemlal prevaricated the answer. Animesh guessed it might be J. Singh who leaked it out because only he knew more about it.

"Won't you be happy that I'm quitting the place?" Animesh asked with a sting remembering how the others ganged up against him only a year and a half ago. He himself was with them because he had to, but not actively.

"No, I will never feel so. I'm never like one of them. I just had to be around and that's all. I can't be nosey, or step into any sort of trouble." He tried to explain. Truthfully, he wasn't like them, he was a simple person. "Yeah, that's true. You're not of that kind, I know. Ok, I'll have a talk with you later." Animesh said and went out to get roties for supper and evening refreshment as well.

The thing was that he had a mutual transfer opportunity a year before but he had refused to take it then because it was not much convenient for him. The school was about ninety kilometers away from his home. What was beneficial was that it was in the suburban Calcutta and it was down the train route. Now he wanted to move out of here at any cost. So, he got ahead.

One month later, it was June. It was the day that he arranged to leave Swallow Nest. The things that would go with him had been packed and tied with rope. The unnecessary things had cluttered a part of the floor of the veranda in front of his door. His room was an extended one on the wide veranda of the mess house.

Animesh called Sujata over. She was the longest lasting maid in Swallow Nest. He gestured at the strewn things of the pile of old newspapers, old books, copies, rough-written bunches of paper, torn up fragile cover files, etc. "You can sell these away and get the money for yourself," he said to her indicating at the clutter. Suddenly his eyes got stuck for one tiny moment on the stapled up four-page handwritten letter that had not been delivered to Anamika, which he had so long kept hidden in a file. Today it came out with the old file.

His thought suddenly ran back to the moment he had waited breathtakingly with Arnab at her door to hand the letter to her. But he was unsuccessful, with bitter humiliating reaction from her. Later on, he learnt that she was married to good engineer which pained him for a long time. Now he didn't think it had any importance any more. He felt it was stupidity of him to preserve such a painful thing so long. "To hell with it," he just thought and planned to tear it into pieces and throw them away into the dustbin, but the phone rang and he went into the room to receive the phone. He spoke to Kartick for about ten minutes. By the time, Sujata cleared away the veranda and he checked if anything forgotten to be packed up. He clean forgot about the letter. Here the fate of the letter changed, so did the story.

PRELUDE

Chapter 1

Somesh Ghosal lived happily in his two-storied house in Dugrapur with his big family after his retirement as a supervisor from Damodar Alloy Steel Plant. He had two sons and a daughter. It'd been three years since Anamika came into this house by marriage with the man's younger son, Bilash. Her parents were so happy and proud to get her married to such a nice groom of such an affluent family. Anamika too was very happy with Bilash; he was a tall, handsome, smart and was an engineer. The first year she had a great honeymoon in marvelous places in Himachal-prodesh and Uttarkhand. The next year they toured across the Andamans and Nikobars. Every year during the Durgapuja vacation they visited some place or the other and enjoyed a lot. In these years she bloomed with better and brighter glamour. One day Bilash mockingly said, "My sweetheart seems to be getting to be a fairy queen on this temporal earth." Anamika smiled amusedly with a reply, "Hell, it's from your pure adoration. I have no intention to reach that high and see people small."

"Does it mean it's only me that adores you? And you don't adore me?" Bilash asked with a mischievous smile.

"Do I have to pronounce it myself? Don't you feel it?" Anamika replied promptly giving a soft pinch at his arm. Here Bilash felt a bit uneasy, not finding a suitable word to it for fun. He said seriously, "I do feel it in every cell in me, baby."

Bilsash pecked at her cheek playfully muttering 'my sweet wife' through his curled lips. At this moment Mohini and Latika got in pushing the door curtain to one side. They both felt uneasy and Biliash got out of the room.

Mohini was Bilash's sister, and Latika the wife of her husband's elder brother. They both suffered the pang of envy at real beautiful Anamika who was at a government-supported job as a high school teacher, while they both were unemployed. It was probably a big reason for them to be envious of her. Anamika, a free-minded and jolly girl, would try to be nice with all of them in the family. She spoke to them freely, spoke funny things, but they didn't seem to accept it freely; and she could feel it. But still she mingled with them with no complexity in her mind.

The first one year went by this way. Now she understood they not only had been keeping distance from her, but many a time dictated to her undesirably. Anamika was intelligent. She thought it would increase by and by, and the relationship with them would turn sour. But it wasn't possible for the couple to buy a piece of land in the costly city and get a new house built so soon. Bilash had still been marking time in his job at a small private company in Calcutta. He was hopeful of getting a good job in govt.-sponsored sector, and then everything would be possible. With hope and patience three years passed through hard times.

One day in the evening Bilash got in home with a broad smile playing across his face and broke the news that he had a great opportunity of going to do an M-Tech in Europe. Anamika was very pleased that her husband was going to achieve a foreign degree, which would be beneficial to him with a good job in the country and she welcomed it with her winning smile. "Man, that's great!" she said, "When are you going?"

"Soon enough", he replied, "May be in two months or less."

"Where will you go?" She asked again. "To Stockholm, in Sweden," He answered. They spent that evening and the next few days with pleasure. Her dream of having a nice house in the city would come true. There reigned an air of happiness and pride in the family. It was natural except Latika. Evnious Latika was discontented but she didn't let it out. Her husband was a clerk at a school whereas her brother-in-law was going to achieve a foreign degree.

Very soon, the pleasure began to die down and soon it brewed some doubt and fear: She heard from her colleagues at school some stories about the people who went abroad were enchanted by those countries and settled out there. This news made her thoughtful: "Will it be good for her or harmful? Europe is so far away. The social culture out there is all different, rather opposite to the Bengalis. Will it happen to him like what they say? What'll happen to me, then? Will he come back at all? Or Will he settle out there? Then what shall I do?" These things kept chasing her.

Two weeks went by with the growing worries. She wished it would be rejected somehow by the authority, but it wasn't. All arrangements were final, even the day he was going to start out. She could no longer hold her from telling him now. She wondered how she would raise the issue. She daringly said out looking at his face, "Can I tell you something?" Bilash looked at her face, "Yes, certainly. Speak."

"Isn't it possible to hold back from your going abroad?" Her hands affectionately twining around his neck slowly, her face was close to his, and her eyes looking into to his eyes attractively. Bilash was surprised at her unexpected request, his hands lightly appealing to loosen her hands, as if to get rid of them from the fearful request, though he didn't move her hands for fear of meaning rude and insulting to her.

"Why, Ana?" he asked in a simple-minded way.

Anamika lightly rested her face by the side of his neck, "I get scared," she said softly.

Bilash couldn't sense the reason for her fear. "Why?" He asked.

Now she brought her face back right over his. "I don't know why, but I do get scared. That's all I know." Her words sounded to him like a demand from a small kid. The other times when she got closer like this, he would feel comfort, and happy, and thought that there was at least someone to take care of him. But now he suddenly felt sort of distant, a bit uneasy. He felt that Europe was beckoning him. How would he kiss it goodbye?

"But you supported me going abroad when I'd first told you about this opportunity!?" He reminded her of the first day's information in a rising tone.

She let herself slip on her back next to him, looking up at the ceiling at the spinning fan. "Yes, I did. Then I didn't feel so."

"Feel what?" he asked and waited for her to answer. Before she answered he repeated, "Feel what? Come on, tell, or else how could I ever know?"

"Feel scared, extremely," she replied putting her face against his side. "Honestly speaking. Please trust me. I feel very much scared."

"But what are you getting scared of, Ana?" He asked with a little emphasis. "Speak your heart out, baby," he demanded. She hesitated to tell the actual reason. "No, I don't want you to go so far away. I just can't let you off."

"It doesn't enter my head what's the reason for your getting scared?" Bilash asked emphatically, kind of confused.

"I told you. I get scared," she prevaricated. "I've got an odd feeling that you shouldn't leave the country."

"Speak point blank." He persuaded. "How come I know unless you make it clear?" He asked sharply.

"I hear they don't let Indian people come back," she replied at last, hesitantly. Here Bilash couldn't help laughing shortly, "Where do you get all this bullshit, honey? Who can hold anyone back if they do want to come back?"

That's the point she thought of. That's why she got concerned. But she couldn't speak over his face what she wanted to. She kept silent for a moment. Then she once again said, "Please, think of me. Who have I got other than you? You are my world. With you so far away and me left out here, how come I live on? I'll be down in the ocean. Try to understand it my way, please." She urged him earnestly.

He tried to understand her pang but now he couldn't stop it. So, he tried to reassure her. "Don't give room for any absurd idea in your heart, my dear. Thousands of people are going abroad to build career or for a job," he said putting his hand on her side. "How can we fulfill our dream, then? We need a lot of money to live well."

Anamika finding not being able to cope up with his reasons, she spoke flatly, "If you can, hold back and forget all about it. I told you what I feel." So saying she once again tried to hid her face into his arm, her hand across his chest, tears burst out and fell on his arm and onto the bed.

Don't worry, my dear, it's a matter of one and half years only. Soon it will be over and I'll come back into your stretched out arms." He turned his head to her ear and half whispered, "I'm always yours, and will be yours for keeps. So long as the sun and the moon will rise in the sky, I'll be yours." He gave a light kiss on her cheek where the tears had run and felt sticky. Anamika stayed passive looking up at the ceiling fan whirling fast, the soughing adding graveness to the dimly lit room. She didn't speak a word.

Bilash realized that she wasn't convinced. He farther said, "Why don't you understand, baby—it's a greater than great opportunity? Not just everybody gets it, nor does it come over and over again."

Anamika took it that she couldn't change his mind about it. "Then promise me, you'll come back as soon as it goes to an end," she demanded for the last time. "You won't forget me. You'll get in touch with me regularly."

Here another gust of tears welled up, and brimmed over and rushed down her cheek. She once again put her face on his chest.

"Of course, I'll come back right away. And I'll always keep in touch with you, speak to you. I'll never ever forget you, Ana. It's a promise," he said moving his hand gently around her back and then cupping her face between his hands, holding his face close to hers, "It's my promise, baby." She was able to take out his words of promise right but still somewhere deep down something out of tune banged since then. She felt sorry that he couldn't relate where she just feared. The night wore on with suppressed discontent in both of them.

Chapter 2

After he'd gone to Stockholm, the couple had a good communication between them for the first year— by writing, or calling on the phone frequently enough. Almost every day either of them made a call spending a lot of bucks on the ISD. But the stubborn concern was eating her away inside as each day passed. She was losing her weight, her face looked dry, her mind was heavy feeling a void in her heart, but she couldn't express it to anybody.

By and by their phoning lessened noticeably. He'd said he would come home after the course was over and go back there again to join the internship course. It goes without saying how pleased she was with the news. She counted the days since the course had four months left to be over. She planned how she would welcome her husband back home, how she would take care of him, what foods of his liking she would cook for him and what foods out of her new recipe she'd make. She had just completed knitting a nice scarf for him for winter use, and a nice half-sweater. She bought a few gifts for him as well. With all these she was looking forward to his way back home. But he didn't come. He joined the one-year's internship instead of paying a short visit to his home. Anamika felt much too sad. She took it to heart and she held back from calling him for the time being saddened anger.

Now she had another trouble that she had to answer about his coming home quite often to the family members. Her father-in-law and mother-in-law both would ask her: "What happened to his coming home? Her sister-in-law, Mohini asked, "When is dada coming home?"

They thought Anamika knew genuinely about his coming back home. Truthfully, she knew the same as they all did. She would answer gravely "I don't know." Sometimes she'd say, "He said he joined the internship. Only that much I've heard." This kind of short answers wouldn't satisfy them. They thought she was avoiding them.

Today as she got into the house from school, Bivarani asked again, "When will he come then? Didn't he say?" Bivarani as a mother would naturally be more restive about her son.

"No," she replied shortly.

"Tell him to come over for a while and go back if he has to," she advised.

Anamika got angry over them all asking her the same questions repeatedly. "Why don't you ask him to come? He's your son. He must obey you, Mother," she answered sharply.

Here Bivarani felt pricked at her sudden sass. "He's your husband as well." She blurted out. Anamika half turned her head toward Bivarani in front of the stairs without an answer thinking that this backchat would lead to arguments and then into a quarrel into a family unrest. She went upstairs with her shoulder bag hanging from her shoulder and a polythene carrier bag from her hand. She got back from school and didn't want get into a quarrel. She didn't have any less load of worries than any other people in the house. Angry Bivarani cast an angry look at her behind as he walked up.

Chapter 3

In the middle of his one-year's internship period, Bilash called Anamika unexpectedly to tell that he was coming home for a time. Anamika was kind of surprised.

Many were the words that Bilash had told her in the meantime were not true. He couldn't keep his promise. So, she couldn't believe his words now. She said, ironically, "Don't try to make fun and fool me. You don't have to come home any longer. Everybody in the home is alright if you were wondering."

From the other side the answer came, "This time I am coming, baby, honest. Trust me."

"Trust you! How many times did you tell the truth like this? Do you remember any?" She countered mockingly with sharpness. She could hear him laugh shortly at her words that seemed to have touched him but he took it lightly. "It's usual it would make you feel bad, get you angry, but I had no way to do anything better while I was far away from home. It was a busy pack of work." He tried to make it light for her. "I'm sorry, very much sorry." He apologized and let out a deep sigh of hopelessness into the phone, which she was able to hear. Anamika felt for the poor chap being so far away living alone.

"Anyway, when if you actually come?" She asked softly.

"During Durgapuja," he answered. "I'm really craving for that festival. I missed three Durgapuja festivals in my native land. And this puja I don't wanna miss out.

"Will you go back there again?" She asked. This question left him in a puzzle. He didn't know how he'd tell her that he would have to go back there again. He stammered a little and hesitated.

"Ye-es, yes, I mean… I have been nearly half the way through the internship. There's still a half left that I'll have to come back for," he replied.

"Then what's the worth coming home in the middle of the internship? Finish the it up and come back for forever. What if you miss out this Puja, too? You'll get the next ones all." Anamika advised. She expected him to come back for keeps bidding good bye to Sweden so there would be no excuse or pull for his going back there.

"In fact, my mind is whirling for my sweet wife, for my parents," he said in appeasement. "I can't settle my mind at work."

"Hell ! You've just said you're coming for Durgapuja! Now you say you're coming for me? I don't believe it," she got him reasonably.

"Yes, both are correct. So, the truth is I'm coming home back to my wife."

Anyway, whatever the matter was, inwardly it comforted her. The talk on the phone on that night was an exciting one. They chatted for so long time that the mobile got hot.

She was happier than she could ever express in words. Now she wouldn't be irritated about being asked about her husband. She'd give them the good news. If you noticed, you could detect a faint smile of happiness always playing in the corners of her naturally pink lips.

At last the day came. A week before Durgapuja, when he turned up, her eyes goggled to see a Swedish girl with him. Her face shrunk in sudden concern. Her heart shook and right away, all the enthusiasm that had been collected in her mind went out like water-vapour out of the spout of a boiling kettle.

"This is my friend," Bilash introduced Anamika with the Swedish girl or rather a woman who seemed older than him. The smart foreign woman was fast with the European etiquette, and she stretched out her hand for Anamika's right away. "I'm Freja, I mean, Freja Nielsson," said the Swedish woman, a big smile on her pink-red face played. But Anamika, in a way, not being as smart as an European, but then was shocked to see a foreigner, held out her hand to Freja but not warmly.

"I am Anamika." She said and observed her carefully. Her blond hair hung down up to her shoulder that shimmered golden as the sunlight fell on it. She was slightly taller than Bilash. In no time, the news of the foreigner passed to the next-door neighbours. People came to see her. It also spread out the Bilash married a foreigner.

From that moment, clouds of doubts and concern began to gather in the sky of her mind. She wondered why he brought her. She thought why ever he didn't tell her that he was brining a Swedish woman with him. Many more things whirled in her intelligent head.

Five-day Durgapuja festival had been over in mixed pleasure for everyone in the house. Then they went out on a tour, especially, in honour of Freja Nielsson for a twelve day visit to a number of scenic places.

It was a few days since the three had come back home from visiting a number of places in Himachal Prodesh, Delhi-Agra, and Uttarprodesh and Madhyaprodesh. During the tour, Anamika couldn't enjoy it like the past years because the foreigner lady around seemed to be watching everything every moment. She couldn't even laugh with her heart out. She kept away from Freja, probably because she couldn't speak English, but then, the European English sounded to her half-pronounced, low-toned and strangled. When Freja wanted to speak to her, she felt very uneasy and replied mostly in 'yes-no' answers. When she praised India a lot after the tour of Northern India, Anamika felt a pinch to her heart, some apprehension in her mind. Under her heart, she felt that Freja ingratiated herself into Bilash. This idea settled in her head like a big stone.

Chapter 4

Bilash went back to Stockholm after the short visit to his home and got to completion of the internship. He kept in touch with his home all right but it lessened again after a few months. The second promise+ Anamika couldn't live in peace after he'd tagged Freja Nielsson along with him and her doubt increased day in day out.

The trouble got around when, after the internship had been finished, he joined Olsson Larsson Company out there. He got the taste of living in a highly developed country in the temperate climate of Europe; it seemed to him no sky was better than that of Sweden, no administration was better than that of Stockholm, and so on. He enjoyed high salary in foreign currency, which was more or less eight times higher than what he'd made in India. Thus, the more he spent in Sweden, the more he liked it, and the more he wished to stay on in there. Here a Bangladeshi friend inspired him to be settled out there explaining the future advantages in Europe and the disadvantages in their own courtiers. If he could have an opportunity of immigration, he'd be able to stay on permanently. It was that guy that first injected the idea of marrying a native girl into him. Bilash'd found it reasonable and futuristic.

Ever since Anamika got to know that he took a job in Stockholm, she became more and more anxious. She often cried into the phone and expressed her helplessness to him. In reply he asked her to go there in Stockholm which, he himself knew well, was not possible for her.

Apprehension grew in her day by day. She impatiently called and asked the most crucial question, "You were to come back home after the whole course was over. Why did you join a company out there?"

He answered, "Working experience in a company is most important for my future opportunities in my country, even anywhere across the world. It's not unknown to you. You have enough sense to realize it." His answer didn't satisfy Anamika or rather it sounded sharp to her. She felt insulted. Anyway finding it reasonable, she went silent for the time being.

After a month or so, she spoke to him and put the same question, 'When are you coming back home?"

He calmly replied as usual, "Be patient, baby. After the year, I'll go back to you." He meant the running year that had five months left.

"Are you honest with your word?" she asked. "Certainly, baby," he answered with a short laugh. "Can't you trust me?" With this story, he went on for a full year.

She counted the year. When she called again, he put up the same excuse to her, "Just one more year, Sweet, and I'll get the immigration here. Once I get it, I can go home any time. And with the immigration I would be eligible to get the citizenship. Everyone said I shouldn't miss out this great opportunity."

She didn't want to hear any more excuses and was going to speak hard but he stopped her, "Listen, listen to me first," he repeated this several times before she stopped.

Look, Ana, for this little impatience, I'll lose the greatest opportunity for ever. After six years, this opportunity has been reopened to Asians. Do you think I should be such a fool to lose it?" Anamika got confused again. She didn't know what to say to it. She didn't want him to work there or get immigration at all. She only asked him how long it would take him to get the immigration, he said "a few months only." Anamika got quiet but inside her went a terrible storm of discontent. Neither she could tell it to anybody nor could she admit it. She remembered her colleagues say that Indians once got into Europe or North America wouldn't get back home.

Days and months went by. Later, 'the few months' came down to 'a few weeks'. Then the 'few weeks' she'd heard for ages. Sensing the ominous indication, she said, "They are just fooling you, dear. Why don't you understand this simple truth?" She wanted to make him realize that he would never get the immigration. She inspired him to quit the job and come back home. Bilash made a short laugh at this thinking that she was conning him. He said, "It's not so, baby. Every nation has some rules for offering immigration to foreigners. So, it takes some time for this complexity. With the immigration today, I will get the citizenship tomorrow."

She felt a blow to her heart inwardly to hear that he was really craving for Swedish citizenship. She couldn't help reacting right away. She said irately, "Why should you be left out there? Come back and get a job here. There are enough opportunities in India."

"Enough opportunities!" he laughed shortly. "You saw them yourself there, before I had this opportunity in Stockholm. Have you forgotten it all?" He tried to refute her persuasion.

She encountered, "But you were not supposed to put down roots in Europe. Then how do you hold this idea today? Am I just nothing to you? What about the promise that you'd made to me?"

He still kept his brain cool at this crucial moment. He calmly described the country as best as he could, perhaps even more than it really was attempting to get her to agree to leave her native India. He further said remembering the Bangladeshi friend's inspiration, "In India there is acute job scarcity and there is no knowing where it'll go in the future. But in Europe there is an ocean-like job opportunities in all walks of life. You too can have a good job here."

She quickly said, "I don't need anything there. I'm alright here with my job in my school."

Once she too had been allured to go there and work. He reminded her, "One day you had asked if there were job opportunities for you, remember?"

She kept silent thoughtfully for a moment, then she said, "It was the past when I didn't know much of the situation. Now I find it is not possible for me to quit my mother here left out all by herself entrusting my sick father to her. And besides, that biting cold is beyond my tolerance." These were the reasons for which she always refused to quit her country. And the clash that had started with an amount first grew bigger and bigger later.

More weeks went by like this with argument and discontent. Anamika couldn't pacify her mind which was getting more and more restive and worried.

The more the time went by, the more he lessened keeping in touch with Anamika—the less he called her or waited for her call. He even wouldn't receive her call then. After her a few calls, he would say, "I was snowed under the pressure of work. Don't mind. In that case, I'll call you back right at my convenience."

She couldn't find it reasonable how a man couldn't just receive the call at that moment and say the few words, "I'm too busy; call you back later." She had to call several times at one stretch to get this answer She couldn't understand how a man could be so cruel.

Today Anamika broke down badly during a long argument on the phone with Bilash as she sensed that she'd not only got away from his eyes but also from his heart. After the call, she confined herself in her room for a long time and shed a lot of tears from the hurt she received.

The more she tried to convince him emotionally, and wept into the phone, the more uneasiness and irritation he felt. And its effect fell in the relationship of the couple. Whenever she'd call on to his phone, he'd be concerned and scared to think what she would ask him, and how he would answer her. He almost stopped speaking on the phone. Anamika was extremely hurt at this sort of behavior that she'd never had from her beloved husband.

From then on, she fell ill quite often from deep concern. She had to take leave from school. Things went topsy-turvy. And each time she fell ill, it worked out worse. She let herself go indifferent about having a good treatment of her illness. Many a time she wept secretly and cursed her fortune. That white-complexioned, blue-eyed, blonde haired Freja had fallen for him and he too let himself slip into it without thinking of innocent Anamika back at home. It was only Freja that brought disaster to her life. This way weeks and months began to pass.

Chapter 5

Good people across the world have always gone through wretchedness or hard times; many have even died untimely. Maybe it is the rule of the universe or maybe God has tested the endurance in them. Anamika being a good girl was no exception either. Only after three years of her marriage, she was thrown into a hell of distress out of her desirable conjugal life. She'd never been in peace ever since Bilash went abroad.

For the past few days, it called ominous in her heart. It made her anxious and stern, which went unnoticed by everyone in the family. She went to school, worked but without zing. She didn't speak much with people around. Questioned by her colleagues, she only said she was not feeling well. How could they know what the hell of a storm was blowing through in her? They advised her as they thought was right.

It was a Saturday. She came back from school early with a headache. She lay down on the bed for a rest and slipped into a nap. She woke at the sounds of the evening rituals but she lazily lay down on the bed half awake, half asleep. Suddenly she could hear something about Bilash through mixed voices from the living room. She pricked up her ears to hear well. Factually, they were talking about her husband's marriage; re-marriage, in fact. It shook her in the heart harder than an earthquake. She kept quiet to hear them better and believe her ears.

"Well, mother, you got a foreign daughter-in-law. Fine," Latika said to Bivarani. Latika was Bilash's elder brother's wife; a secret soft villain in the house.

"It's no pleasure for me; maybe for you." Bivarani reacted with emphasis. A mother-in-law from the pure village culture would never like the ways of foreign women. So, she wasn't supposed to be pleased and she really wasn't. And besides, she loved Anamika a bit more than

Latika. That's where was Latika's irritation over Anamika. From day one, she was kind of envious about Anamika. She made her feel it several ways at different times directly or indirectly. But, because of the goodness in Anamika, she didn't let it touch her beneath. Or rather she tried to be on her best behaviour with everybody.

Naturally, Latika was pleased inwardly about the news; "Why, mother, you can occasionally visit foreign countries and me too, if you tag me along with you, however. You'll tell proudly, 'I'm going to my son's house in Europe,'" Latika said ironically.

"Yeah, I'm already with one step out, huh?" Bivarani said in an ironical disapproval. "I know they are man eaters." With a pause she added, "No, no, Bilash did very wrong to have married that undisciplined girl. I'll tell him to come back home right away. I don't need money from there. I want my son back home."

Latika farther said, "When he has done it incidentally, admit her in the family, mother. Or else, there will be a family unrest," She persuaded her with words poured into her ears like Monthora did to Koikee in the epic of Ramayana. "You keep your mouth shut." Latika finding her angry over her quickly said, "Okay, I shut my mouth."

"I'll never ever give her admission in here, remember," Bivarani issued a warning. "He too, will be very angry when he hears about it." She meant to mention Bilash's father, Somesh Ghosal.

It was then Anamika turned up before them anxiously, her eyes looking at their faces searchingly. They were busy watching the few pictures of the marriage on Latika's mobile. They calmed down suddenly to see her and looked at one another. She looked at the mobile eagerly in Mohini's hand. "What happened, didi? What pictures are you all watching?" She asked looking up at Latika and then at Mohini, and stretched her hand for the mobile, but Mohini turned sideways and kept on watching them expressing her surprised reactions on the familiar Freja. Mohini was Bilash's sister, tan-skinned, average-looking girl, still unemployed for two years after she'd completed the M.A.

THE DESTINED DESTINIES 203

Anamika turned to Latika and asked again, "What happened? Tell me, please. Tell me." She prayed.

Bivarani, who had crossed the doorstep into the room came back to them and quickly said out, "Nothing, honey, nothing. Don't worry. You get in and rest." She turned to Latika and Mohini, and said, "Don't speak anything absurd. It'll breach the peace in the family."

Anamika caught it and was sure something had happened. She looked at Latika and then at Mohini, and then at her mother-in-law.

"Don't hide it from me. Tell me please," Anamika prayed to them all. "I'm strong enough to face it."

"No, no, nothing happened. You go inside," Bivarani said nervously again and pressed her to move in. But Anamika didn't care for her words. Her only aim was to know the secret.

Latika proved once again with her suppressed chuckle that she envied her and was pleased at the grand accident to Anamika's life. It was Latika, who blurted out the truth at that moment. "Your Bilash has married the Freja Nielsson. Do you remember her? See the photos." She indicated at the mobile when Bivarani called in a threatening tone staring at her angrily, "Latika?" and she tried to take the mobile from Mohini, but Anamika snatched it, and turning away, she stepped off and gazed down at the marriage pictures. Latika wasn't anxious for her mobile instead of Bivarani's prohibition, or rather she waited for her to see the pictures well and believe that it was true.

"What did you do, Latika?" Bivarani complained with annoyance, "You blurted it out stupidly?"

Latika felt insulted at the pricking word 'stupidly' and reacted: "It's no use being so anxious about it. Don't you think you could hold it back! Sooner or later, she would get it, certainly. Everybody would know of it."

Anamika was still staring at the pictures. Her eyes broke into tears. "How come you did this? Oh, Lord!" She pronounced weakly with tons of sadness. "Is that what I had to see? Oh Lord!" She felt dizzy and began to see stars in her eyes and tottered but before she fell down Latika and Mohini grabbed her and sat her down on the couch behind them. There was a usual noise of calling one another. Everybody got busy nursing her. Mr Somesh Ghosal woke up from the noise, and came out hurriedly. He too got shocked to learn about his son's re-marriage.

Anamika came round after a while, right, but the shock did a lot of harm. She felt too weak to stand up. She wept bitterly until she made herself sick again. Truthfully, there's nothing more horrible to a woman than losing all her rights over her husband. She bonded her heart to Bilash and there was no way she could take it back. A Hindu woman out of the pure village culture could never keep from being shocked deeply at this accidental occurrence. She cursed her misfortune and also herself over and over again for her failure that she couldn't convince him into coming back to India after he'd gone through the courses out there. She went on weeping through consolations from her family folks including Latika's dry, slapdash, heartless consolation.

Chapter 6

Since that day, she changed a lot. She would always be tensed and disappointed and angry. She lived as if she was indifferent to herself, not caring what went on around her. And with days going by, she fell ill more often, and more seriously. At the same time, she neglected her treatment in spite of the family folks' advices. But she would mostly hear them in one ear and out the other, or sometimes she would say, "I don't need any. I'm alright." Inwardly she wanted to mean: "What's the use of all these? When the life has turned valueless, I don't want to live anymore." This way she passed the days with illnesses and recoveries.

Early winter, she fell seriously ill. She had to be admitted to Jupiter Multi-privilleged Hospital. High sugar, stomach ulcer, liver trouble and low pressure ringed her up. She broke down badly because during her week-long stay in hospital, her Bilash didn't call her for once to know about her. Bilash had the news of her from his mother or from Latika or Mohini. In fact, he didn't have the face to face her directly because of his guilty-consciousness. Here she concluded that not only did he avoid her but also deleted her from his mind and wanted to get rid of her. This was another hurting impression to her. Lying on the hospital bed, she wept deeply and wiped tears that rolled down her cheeks unnoticed. But her mother, Minatirani saw this. Sitting beside her, she moved her hand along her head. "All will be alright, honey. Keep faith in God. He'll put things right again," She said to comfort her.

"I've lost everything, mum. How come I live in that house?" She asked helplessly, her voice broke and her martyred eyes melted again. Tears welled up in her mother's eyes, too.

"You don't have to think of it right now. Be released from the hospital. Then I'll take you home for better treatment." She consoled her, but Anamika didn't feel reassured and remained silent looking up at the ceiling. Minatirani farther added wiping the tears of the corners of her eyes, "Don't break down like this, honey. You have to live and see yourself as the winner. You have to be firm in mind." Anamika let her head roll to the other side on the white pillow with a sigh of depression out. She closed her eyes and lay quiet; the mother held her daughter's hand in hers thinking deeply.

Chapter 7

Twelve years was no less amount of time out of one's golden period of life. It was that long that Bilash had been away from Anamika. She'd suffered a lot of illness from anxiety through these years. With Minatirani's careful care and affection, she'd recovered physically in full here at her father's home in her lived-in turf. Again she commuted to her school regularly as she used to, again she sat around and chatted with her colleagues, neighbouring boudies (=elder brothers' wives) and sisters, and had fun. They would come over to her or she would go to them at leisure. She was also a jolly girl to make a lot of fun for them to enjoy. All the same, the soar of the anguish inside her burning like a soft flame didn't seem to be tamed; something inexpressible pained her in the heart and she covered it up somehow with her strengthened mind. Just as, an oyster would cover a tiny painful grit in its body with its sticky juice to form it into a pearl, the same way, Anamika would wrap her pains in her determination and let it out in the fun and jolliness. Just as many people didn't know that the pearl was the result of the lengthened pain in the oyster, like so, they didn't know her jolliness resulted from the suppressed pain in her heart.

Minatirani would often be worried thinking about her daughter's future and talked about it to the ones she was close to, but not to her daughter; she'd get angry about it. But, still, one day she dared say to her daughter, "Honey, call him once, write to him; keep in touch with him. Learn how he is or what he's doing." The mother and the daughter were watching a movie together then. In connection with the movie, she said so. Anamika's lips got firm, and her face turned grim staring at her mother's face but she heard her out. "I know it sounds irritable to you, but still believe me—things will be alright again. God will smile at you."

She would always be angry at her mother's begging attitude towards Bilash. She said, "Mum, has your daughter fallen into the gutter or into the fathomless ocean that she has to run after a deceiver crying for his pity?"

Minatirani lost her tongue for the moment and held her confused look at her daughter's face as her daughter went on, "I haven't broken the conjugal bondage; it's him that did it. So, it's his duty to glue it up, not mine. And besides, listen up, mother, after so many years, I'm not gonna get back to him. I have come across these many years, and I will pass the future years all right, as well, God willing."

"You can't understand one thing," Minatirani still tried to convince her; "a woman can't live secured without her husband."

"Oh, of security if you mean, you got me married to him for security, what the hell of it has he done?" she questioned reasonably. Minatirani went silent at this, so did Anamika for a moment. Then she farther said, "I make enough money than I know what to do with it? I have no problem to live on all by myself freely with it. If you had an eye, you'd find many more women living alone with so little money." With a pause she said again, "Listen up, Mum, to my eyes he's no better than a traitor. He can't expect any better from me; and that's flat."

Minatirani felt sad that her educated daughter wouldn't try to realize it. So, she kept wordless for a moment and then she said weakly, "Okay, do as you think is good for you." She heaved a deep sigh of hopelessness and walked out towards the kitchen slowly.

More time went by with her thought of determined freedom at her father's home. The health and the glamour that had gone down badly were made up much of it, except for the suppressed pain of 'what it all had been and what has it just turned out to be'.

Chapter 8

The global warming affected the weather noticeably—the rains wouldn't come in time, or shower enough rain, the Kalboishakhi storms were about to be extinct, the summer would be unbearably ruthless, winter wouldn't come in time and last enough or wouldn't be cold enough, but the morning today looked similar to the one that had come fifteen years back. It dewed heavily on the plant-leaves, water droplets dripped from them onto the ground, the grass looked white like silver pearls, water-vapour rose up from the pond behind the house, layers of fog floated over the open green field. Truthfully, they all made a wonderful typical ambience of a pre-winter season. It felt typically cold as then. People usually wouldn't feel this ambience unless they were conscious about the natural beauty.

The sun just came up the horizon in the south-east. Having brushed her teeth, washed her hands and face, and having had her tea in her upstairs room, she was in the middle of looking over the answer papers of the test examinations.

Minatirani walked into her room, stood beside her chair for a while looking down at her examining the answer sheets sitting at the table. Before she spoke, she picked the used cup and saucer in her hand and put the other hand on the back of the chair, still in hesitation. "What would you prefer to eat today, honey?" She asked, sort of fearfully because in the last years she always protested about this question.

"What I'll eat?" she asked back looking up at her mother's face quizzically, the red pen held in her hand. The tone of her question almost gave the answer. Minatirani felt a bit uneasy at this.

"Have you forgotten it's the fifteenth anniversary?" Minatirani asked.

"Yes, I have, because I should," she said grimly. She certainly didn't forget the day. What woman could ever forget the best ever date of her life? It did prick her in the morning and the pent-up pain wanted did break out of its cover and make her sad but she managed it.

Minatirani was an intelligent, a down-to-earth woman. She didn't want that the relationship made in front of a holy-fire be denied or deleted. Once married, one can't terminate it like weeds in the crop field. She said, "Fifteenth anniversary is a mile-stone for a marriage. So, I kind of, thought of cooking something special—fried rice, castrated-goat meat, and coconut prawn...."

"No, mum, nothing any of these, please!" she said putting her hands together with the pen in them in a begging attitude. "Just veg-dishes or fish as usual. Don't be sad, mum."

"But I have already ordered for the meat and prawn. What will happen to them? What should I do now?"

"Cancel them all. Why did you do so without asking me?" Anamika asked annoyingly.

There was an evident picture of disappointment on Minatirani's face. Anamika noticed it and felt bad for her. She wanted to soothe her. "Mum, can you enjoy the food that has gone stale, or wear the garland that has rotten, or a garment that has shattered torn?" She asked and looked up at her face to know if her mother related her. Minatirani related her right. She didn't spend any more words on this matter. She walked out and down the stairs silently with the cup and saucer clinking in her hand.

She understood she left her mother in saddened thought. She dropped the pen on the answer sheet that had been half way through and leant back in the chair, her chin cupped by her hand. For some time she got lost in thought, too. Then she said out, "To hell with it. To hell with everything. Every man is unkind and selfish. Let the world go to hell." She got up onto the bed and lay down with no pillow under her chest, her head down on the bed. Once again she breathed out, "To hell with the world." Tears streamed out of her eyes.

Chapter 9

The spring, the summer, the rains went. Also the autumn was about to go because they had to. Anamika hardened her heart even more. She didn't step into her father-in-law's since she'd left that house. In the mean time, Mohini was married, she was invited. Somesh Ghosal passed away, she was given this news. But she didn't call to them herself. She'd thought she didn't belong to that family anymore and it would be immoral to thrust herself to call them. She completely isolated herself from that family, in fact. These were the things she was thinking as she was coming back home from the market. The evening darkness was coming closer all around, the far-off trees were silhouetted against the twilight after the sundown at the horizon. It was a melancholic scene. Concluding with "forget the world" she walked in when her mother asked her to offer the evening rituals. She nodded and walked upstairs.

She put down the jute bag on the bed. It had two Student's Attendance Registers and four quires of white paper sheets and ruled paper sheets in two rolled-up packs.

Changing into ritualistic saree, she lit up the oil lamps and incense sticks before God in the attic temple and showing them all around the house and before the basil plant (tulsi) in the yard, she bowed down for God's bless and put them where they ritually belonged to.

Then changing out of the ritualistic costume, she stood by the bed and unwrapped the covering of the two rolled packs. One of the wrapping paper-pieces showed the name 'Anamika' on its top before her, swaying in the fan wind. It was a turning point but she didn't notice it.

She put the four quires of paper straightened up on her table when Minatirani got in with the evening tea in her hand. As she took it in her hand, her mother said, "The gas is burning low. Has it really run low so soon or the burner is disturbed?"

"Who knows?" she was in confusion. Then she looked at her mother. "It's not long since the new one has been put on. It's not supposed to run low so early!" Anamika said in logical conclusion, holding the saucer in her hand and sitting in her chair close to the bed, Minatirani standing behind her. "Then call somebody to see to it," Anamika suggested.

She started having tea with cookies. The two pieces of the junk paper swayed by the fan-wind behind her and then were blown off the bed under the old-fashioned bedstead bidding goodbye to the other two pieces that wrapped the two registers on the bed.

A long time passed. She drank the tea slowly, put away the jute bag of the register books to carry them to school, did some personal work, watched TV, chatted with her mother, and helped her with cooking supper, then she ate, and finally went to sleep.

The next morning was a holiday, so Anamika was at home. Hena was sweeping the room out while she, sitting in her chair, was directing her to sweep better where she thought wasn't done properly. "Get that corner well, Hena," she said pointing towards the spot, "and... yeah, get in farther, yeah still farther." She indicated under the bedstead. Hena tried to do it as she directed. "See, what a lot of dirt is coming out," she said. "These days you are faking your duty a lot, Hena," she said complainingly.

"Yeah, I am. You always find faults in me, no matter how good I do," Hena sassed back playfully. She worked in this house for many years and became like a member of the family. So, they behaved with her and she with them sort of freely or funnily. "Don't argue. I have seen you fake your duty with a little chance," Anamika said plainly, watching over her sweeping. Hena worked without talking back now. She half got in under the bedstead and swung the broom in a half circle up to the wall underneath and swept all that came in its range and one of the wrapping papers of the last night came out near her chair with its front side up. It was then her eyes fell on the words, *'Dearest Anamika'*. That did it. Right away, it shot a jerk beneath her chest. Her name written in a style shook her beneath. "What's that paper? Pick it up, pick it up," she told Hena sort of impatiently, pointing to the sheet and leaning down from her chair.

Hena picked it, dusted it and rubbed it lightly on her dress to shake off dust and pieces of hair from it. She took it in her hand and read the name again carefully. It was the front page of a letter. She understood where it was from, and remembered the past about it. It dated back to a little more than eighteen years.

"There is another piece, should I pick it or sweep it away?" asked Hena while sweeping.

Anamika stretched out her hand, "Give me that one too." She then tallied the sequence of the writing and was sure there were more pages. "Is there any?"

"No," Hena replied and continued. She waited for Hena to move away sweeping from the bedstead. Then she got up and unwrapped the register pack as well. Yes, there were two more pages. She put all the four pages together. The letter was ended by Animesh Bhabook. Right away she remembered him sending her the New Year Greetings Card which she'd returned.

At first she felt abhorrence to recall his name and the past but curiosity pushed her forward. Or else she wouldn't have given it a damn about it at all; but because she had been separated from her family, she felt a desperate curiosity about it.

It was a four-page letter, the longest one she'd ever known of. The pages of the letters had been crumpled and torn in places. She straightened them up carefully and put them in order.

She waited until Hena left the room after mopping the floor. She would have to know what it was all about.

Chapter 10

When the time is ripe for you to deserve something, it comes to you one way or the other. It was true with Anamika. Ultimately, it reached her, but by then, it was too late for both, the sender and the receiver.

Anamika closed the doors and bolted them and lay on her belly on the bed, a pillow under her chest. It was the first time ever she was going to read such a letter. She never knew what it felt like to get a long letter from a man. So, she was eager for it and felt jumpy. She swallowed and started reading the handwritten letter:

Dearest Anamika,

My earnest request—please, get through this letter with a little time out of your busy day—but, in secret, of course. This is the first time ever in my life I'm writing a letter of deep, heartfelt feeling to a girl friend, and it's to you. So, keep your great heart open and take it easy, will you?

After I'd watched you for a moment at the end of the final exam-day on the 1 July, I came back to Burdwan. God in heaven knew how I ever tried to get in touch with you. It may sound an exaggeration to you, but I did, honest. Your place is in Kanchannagar I know—beyond the city, but still my restive, anxious eyes looked around in the hope of grabbing a look at you by some coincidence, but it went in vain; I couldn't see you.

Anamika, you ain't surely forgotten that I'd sent you messages many times during those days, but I was certain that they had been delivered distorted to you. I could have faced you direct but didn't dare; for fear of being hurt badly or defamed out of any chaos. Truthfully, dignity-conscious people wouldn't dare. Anyway, let it be dropped.

Frankly to speak, Anamika, I liked you soon after I'd met you on the very first day of the session. I watched you every day—your movement, your behavior, your humane feeling, your choice of words, even your sweet jolly wickedness with humour. The liking deepened by and by; I didn't know when I placed you in the core of my heart. Your skilled singing impressed me specially, although I didn't have an opportunity of learning to sing, but I love songs very much and often hum to myself. The indomitable love for you made it easy for me to tune up with the Tatanic's Oscar wining song. In the end, the stage fright held me back from singing it on the stage in the annual function.

My New Year greetings card to you containing a six-line English poem when you'd sent back to me, I got to know once again how simple you were. But your returning the card touched me beneath. Truthfully, I was bewildered. Because I'd gone so far that there was no way back. Is that why I've been having this distress so much? Is this the punishment for me for that? I was wondering.

Anamika, you may ridicule or look down on me like what your friends did because they infected you with their own vanity but still I can't help wishing you the best, always, because it's you who's the first one out of my emotional feeling from the bottom of my heart. One thing keep in mind, dear, don't try to look at anybody with other people's eyes; it won't come out to be the right evaluation. If you've had any bad ideas or feelings about me, only the charmed circle around you got it to you distorted. I'm sure they did it. Once I read a book: How to Read a Person Like a Book; a very useful book that helped me read one's body language. In fact, every person's thought would come out in their attitude, in their movement, and in their faces. You never got to know me because it never occurred to. Think it over in the serenity, you'll find the answer.

It's my fortunate misfortune that people have most often got me wrong, and they've accused me of what I didn't deserve. That pent-up pain that accumulated day by day formed into a poem one day which was: *Left out on the Shore*. You may have read it in the college magazine. It didn't mean I love to be alone; it was a reflection of regret against the unjust accusations. Please, don't accuse me wrongly like they did. Any complaints, tell me direct. To know the truth is the act of intellectuality. If I have made any mistakes, they have only occurred unknowingly. Pardon me for that, please.

On the last exam day, I wanted to see you outside the exam centre and hand over the annual function photos I'd promised you, but unfortunately I was a bit late to come out of the exam hall and you a bit earlier. When I came out hurriedly, I saw you walking in a jolly mood with your friends along the stone-less, grass-covered, narrow-gage track and me following you far behind fruitlessly to catch up with you.

I had to go up to you at your hostel to keep my promise and to tell you something but I noticed you were much too grave, and myself rather too anxious and nervous. Standing at the crux, not only did I lose my words but also my guts. Having given you your photos and my card, I asked to you to give me a call because you said you didn't have a phone so that I could have called you. Since then many days went by with the sun up in the sky and down the skyline and me expecting a call, but Anamika's phone didn't come. I consoled myself: a girl would find it to be the hardest thing to call a man. But more to the point, I sometimes wondered if I cried for the moon or I actually deserved a call from you. All the same I hoped if you'd give me a call, at the least for once!

I still didn't know why you stood before me with that darkened face at your hostel gate—if only you'd told me the reason!

I don't usually do any wrong consciously; it's not my characteristics to hurt anybody. Or rather, I'm a shock absorber I believe. If I have shocked you anyway, forgive me. What I believe strongly is I'm simple enough. May be simplicity is the reason for my miseries in many ways, and I'm having the punishment. Whatever punishment I have to take,

I will, but I can't be a cunning or coaxing or selfish man, a deceiver or a drunk.

I will admit the sanctioned fortune for me in the roll of the rules of the grand universe. Tagore said, "If the Supremo on high smiles at you, each and every thorn blooms into a flower, every spot of mud turns into a sandal prolep and all the defame to be enlightened..." If God's not with you, you can't succeed in anything. When the fortune itself appears to be an enemy, everybody finds faults in you, everything is bungled up.

Will you too, look down on me like some others? If I have committed a crime to have dreamed about you in my heart, then I should swear, I committed a lot of crimes to have willed to be working in Akashvani Kolkata radio, or to have willed to work abroad in the Western World. I spent up my good money in those dreams for years. These are my temptation or ambition, whatever you may call them. I still have them alive, and will have them tomorrow. So, once these lines came out of my thought:

I'm rich, I am rich—
Yes, rich in greed
Some good ambitions I do breed.
So, I run after
What is farther
Or beyond my catch;
Rich in greed, I am I watch.
I'm rich, I am rich—
Yes, rich in dream.
So, I dare swim
In an unreal stream.
I get drifted and sink later;
No shame, I get filled with water!
Back to sense when I get
All is lost; it's too late.

At the end, its' an urge to you—give me a little time, please, only to speak my heart out for a moment, It's so important that I have to speak to you to make myself free from the tightened squeeze of the strong anxiety:

And after that,
If you must,
Shower on me as hard
With your final word
From your lips.
I'll take that blow
With a secret sigh
And be calm for keeps.

Or else there is no way to my salvation from this torment in my poor heart.

Yes, I do love Anamika. I do love you, Anamika, with all my heart. I'll keep on loving you for keeps. I could never ever get out of that love. The truth of all truths is:

Whom I have taken deep down into my heart,
Have been worshipping so intently,
Even if the earth and planets stop,
Let them,
Or the stars all burn out
Or the springs all dry out,
Let them—
How come I forget her?
I have loved Anamika is the truth,
If nobody knows matters not,
My heart knows better
And He on high.

I look forward to seeing you for a moment at the least or a phone-call on this number 0206, 1311969. Stay lucky.

Sincerely yours

Animesh Bhabook

When she'd got through the long letter, a deep sigh went out; she remained uncharacteristically calm, gazing down at it, and then she put her head down on her folded arms, a part of the letter underneath, her eyes streaming down with tears. A number of past scenes came crowding before her closed eyes—how her friends composed an anti-Animesh ambience around her, how she held the New Year greetings card and how she sent it back to him, and so on. Her eyes shed a lot of tears; drops of them fell onto the letter.

When she raised her head, through her blurred eyes, she noticed the tear drops wetting the letter. She dried them carefully with her shash end and held it to her chest. Her heart became heavy as if the weight of the whole earth had fallen on it.

In the last few days she read the letter a few times and began to think differently. The more she read it, the more effect it cast in her mind; the more she realized how much he loved him. She felt guilty now. She wished she could fly over to him like a bird and bow down to him asking to be forgiven for her misbehaviour!

Seeing abnormality in her for a few days, Minatirani one day asked, "What's wrong with you, honey? Are you sick?" She felt her forehead to check for fever.

"Nothing wrong; I'm alright," Anamika replied with a short artificial laugh. Her mother holding an observing look at her face said, "No, I don't think you're all right. Tell me the truth."

She felt uneasy to have been caught and felt like getting out of her mother's sight as soon as could be. "I'm alright," she repeated it weakly and turned her head and went upstairs. Minatirani couldn't know what happened to her. It was only Lord and she herself knew what had been going on in her.

Chapter 11

It was a Thursday of July. The setting sun turned the clouds colourful with multi colours over the horizon. Anamika turned up at Swallow Nest. She had a boy of eight years with her.

She felt her heart throbbing abnormally beneath her chest. The mild July breeze seemed to be whispering into her ears; the noise and the honking of the vehicles giving her a strange intuition. She felt her face dry, radiating warmth.

She was on a mission with a faint hope of meeting somebody there. She held back at a little distance from the main door of the mess staring at it. She watched mess-boarders getting in back from work through the main door. She still dilli-dallied from hesitation. After some time, suddenly remembering the time, she looked back at the colourful western sky. She found that the sun had just set, the colours of the sky had faded. She'd have to go a long way back home. The job that she got out for had to be done quickly. So, she plucked up courage and walked up to the door with hesitant steps from inexpressible feeling. She could now hear the loud talk of some boarders.

She knocked on the door and waited looking down. No reply came. She knocked once again. A woman's voice came from inside, "The door's open."

She heard it but still didn't feel easy to walk in. So, she knocked once again. Umanath, the cook of the mess told Sujata to get the door.

As the door opened, Anamkia saw a very ordinary woman in a saree looking curiously at her face. It was Sujata, the maid for the mess. "Mean to say something?" She asked Anamika wondering about the beautiful woman at the door.

"Ye-ye-es," Anamika said, gulping down. Sujata saw the kid standing beside her. "Does Mr Animesh Bhabook live here?" She asked.

"Oh, him? He's gone away a long time ago." Sujata replied.

Just as a big explosion thrusts a gust of air from a loud bang across the face, so did it to her heart to hear of him 'gone long ago'. This is what she'd feared of.

"A long time ago!" Anamika breathed out with a short sigh of hopelessness and she half leaned her head thoughtfully, not knowing what to do. Sujata didn't miss her despair. "Where are you coming from?" she asked.

Anamika answered, "Kanchannagar."

By the time the cook, other members at the kichen called, "What's up? What's the matter?"

"She wants to see Animesh-babu." Sujata said loudly.

"Tell her to come in," the secretary called.

Anamika followed Sujata into the yard hesitantly. A chair was brought out and offered to her to sit down on the concrete yard but she didn't sit. She thanked them instead. The kid was standing beside her. Because she was a woman in an unknown place, they didn't persuade her to sit down any more.

"Anyway, talking about Animesh-babu, you wanted to see him—but he doesn't live here anymore. He left the mess more than a year ago," said the secretary and others. A few more boarders from upstairs came down from curiosity. "In fact, he got transferred after a lot of attempts; to Jeerat." She listened silently.

Both the parties stayed silent for a moment, when the cook said out, "Animesh-babu was real nice, amicable man—a gentle, reticent, polite and kind-hearted person. Anyone mingling with him for some time will like him and love him, I bet. He was such a good, gentle, kind and jolly man."

"Do you know his address there, or his contact number?" Anamika asked shyly.

"Yes, contact number can be given from our register, but his address—" the secretary paused, "yes, Mahato took his address. If you can wait a while, you'll get him. He will be right in, supposedly."

Anamika found that it wasn't possible for her to wait. She said, "I'll get the address later. If possible, you can give me the phone number, please."

"Let's see." Some of them busily searched for his number.

"Tomorrow is Friday. Most of us will be out for home. No problem; you can get it from the cook." He tossed his hand at the cook who was sitting on the kitchen veranda resting a while after he had been back from his outdoor work. "Yes, you can come after five and get it, or in the morning till half past nine."

After she'd left the mess with the phone number, there went a curious talk and comments about Animesh and Anamika. Different boarders thought variously about them, but Anamika got back home with worries, wondering how she would find him. She too had to say something to him.

THE DESTINED DESTINIES
Part- Two

The second turning of the story

Chapter 1

It was a holiday in the middle of the week for the Mahalaya. Goddess Durga is welcomed on this day. Usually, he went home on this day to enjoy listening to the Mahalaya on the radio half-asleep and half-awake on the bed at dewy dawn. But God might have had another plan for him and He held him back from going home. He listened to the Mahalaya here on the mobile from Akashvani Kolkata (radio station).

All day long today, he had a queer feeling in his mind but there was no clear indication. Anyway, he got along with his work doing usual things. He did some reading on spirituality. He'd started listening to music again since he came to Jeerat. He listened to some music, as well. Each song of the particular past times reminded him of the particular situations of decades before. Lunch was over. He sat at his computer watching a movie but soon the lunch-driven siesta got him; he went into a drowsy state swaying like a branch in the breeze, the movie was going on.

Suddenly he half startled out of his drowsiness hearing the tintinnabulation of the newly installed electronic calling bell. He wondered about the ring; nobody was to come at this odd time. The electrician was due to come next day; the gasman delivered the new gas this morning. Wondering who it could be, he lazily stood up from his chair and crossed the dining room to the door.

Just as he opened the door, he got real astounded to see a beautiful lady at his door-step looking up at his face smiling slightly with shyness. Animesh's eyes goggled; it was the face he could never ever forget in his life, it was the face once he couldn't tear his eyes away from—it was Anamika standing unbelievably before him! His drowsiness vanished in a second. For a moment he was bewildered. He couldn't speak right away; the sudden surprise got his nerve stiff.

"This is the Anamika! Why has she come!?" He thought, flabbergasted. At this crucial moment a strange fear began to creep into her mind and she began to feel uneasy. Slightly puzzled, her lips parted to say something when Animesh said out loud, "Oh, my God! Who do I see at my door?" His excited exclamation even surprised her as well and dispelled her fear of being insulted by his carelessness about her. "Anamika is here! I can't believe my eyes, honest," he exclaimed with the same excitement. "How are you, Anamika? How did you find me out? Where are you coming from? How did you get this address?" He asked a number of questions in one breath and she didn't know what to answer to which question. In the deep of her mind words bobbed up—"I've got a lot to say but I wonder how I will." Instead she said, "Can't you forgive me, Animesh-da?" and looked up to his face intently for his answer.

Animesh didn't answer to her vital, crucial question right away; instead, he let out a plain smile and said, "Won't you come in? Or will you just say goodbye at the threshold?"

"How come I, unless you ask me to?" She asked back.

"Oh, yes, certainly. Please, come in." He welcomed her taking one step back. He led her into the living room of his rented house and offered to sit in the couch. He called the maid over as he sat himself down in the other couch in a ninety degree angle. They sat facing each other. The maid of about forty-five years was doing the dishes in the kitchen. As she came over, he ordered for some heavy refreshment from the market in spite of Anamika's protest. By the time she looked around the room. She could see the clutter in the living room and also on the bed of the bedroom that she could see through the open door. She realized how a solitary life of a bachelor's could be. She felt for this poor man.

For a moment—both of them seemed to be in thought and couldn't speak. Animesh watched her intently. He noticed the small spot of vermilion i.e. *sindur* in the parting of her hair and gold-banded conch bangles on her wrists. He thought, "It's the same Anamika of about two decades ago. She has changed a little. She was a young woman then; slimmer, now a married middle-aged woman; gained some weight but beauty has been the same," while Anamika watched his changes that came through the long years in his face and hair. She wondered how she would say what she wanted to tell. The situation was rather hard to tackle for her. Minute parts of time kept ticking by. Anamika looked down at her restive hands and then at Animesh's face shyly. Inwardly she was shivering from tension thinking of her mission, why she came which was kind of an adventure to her. Somewhere in her heart she thought if she did it right to have come a long way up to here. However, it was no use thinking of it now.

Her sweet voice that once sounded like the wind chimes to him one day didn't seem to sound that way now. That he had wanted to speak to her for once so badly and listen to her last words didn't seem to be anything today. Once her beauty seemed filled up with the world's whole beauty didn't seem that way now. The thing is that when your stomach is ready to take food, the food tastes good, when your mind's eager to listen to something, it sounds real sweet to your ears. Animesh came a long way past the period and his liking changed. He was in another world now. All the same, he was more pleased than he could ever say.

"There you are," Animesh began. "Come on, take it easy, Anamika." Animesh said out first. "What made you come up to here after so long time, so far away?" There was a slight pricking touch in it, although he didn't mean to prick her; it just came out in the flow of the sentence because he never was a good speaker. In fact, he was more pleased than he could ever say. "First tell me, 'how you are you?" she said and looked at his face for his answer.

Animesh said plainly, "I'm alright. Mustn't grumble, I should say—working, eating and sleeping. That's all. But let mine be dropped. Tell me about you," he demanded.

Her head half bent forward with shame. She looked down at her twined fingers rubbing slightly. Animesh noticed it, too. "That's a long story to tell, Animesh-da," she said in a small voice. "I'm more sorry than I can ever say that I couldn't empathize with you in time. Now I did," Anamika swore hesitatingly.

Here Animesh raised his eyebrows in curiosity. He got a jerk under his chest to hear the phrases 'long story', and 'empathize with you'. He could well realize that she spoke from the core of her heart, but he wondered why so, what happened, especially after so many years!

Before he asked about it, Anamika mentioned the undelivered letter addressed to her from Animesh. He was surprised at this. "How strange!" exclaimed in surprise and stirred in his couch, his eyes widened. He remembered the day when he looked down at the letter with the junk he'd taken out of his room and let it go before he'd left Swallow Nest. He also remembered he was to have torn it into pieces, which he'd forgotten. But he could no way figure out how it reached her hand; how this miracle happened. On asking, she explained it all.

Animesh was more surprised at this. He exclaimed again, "It's such a coincidence! It's hard to believe! Really!" Suddenly, his thought ran farther back to Arnab—the scene at her door floated before his eyes once again. How Arnab tried to convince him several times to come back to normal life when the letter hadn't been delivered and Animesh was extremely upset. But he couldn't admit the convincing.

He lowered his head. "The letter reached her at last! How is it possible? Is that God's will, or something more than that?" he thought to himself.

Disrupting his trance Anamika said, "I have got through the letter several times. I have known you afresh through the letter, Animesh-da. I've known you as a real good person with all class in you. Since then, you don't know how I've felt about you. I couldn't sleep well. That's why I've rushed over to you to apologize. Or else I couldn't pass a day in peace." With a pause she said, "Can't you forgive me, Animesh-da?" she urged.

"I've always forgiven you, honey." Animesh said feelingly, "You'll always be dear to me, and a true friend—you know why?" He paused shortly. Anamika felt more eager to listen to his explanation. "Because I knew you had no fault of your own. I knew it was certain friends of yours that you'd been encircled by. It was them that propelled you, and didn't let you think your own way, didn't let you look out over the wall they built around you and didn't let you know the truth beyond the wall. And, your innocent mind, however, didn't want to get over the barrier either."

Here tears welled up in her eyes. She said, "It was my bad, and my bad luck, I swear. That's why I'm here to apologize." Animesh watched her lean her head down and blink her eyes several times trying to hide the tears.

"Why do you regret, Anamika? You're lucky you've had a good, highly qualified husband with a plum job abroad. You've got a happy life with your own plum job with the real economic freedom. You should be happy." He tried to soothe her.

"I've already told you, it's a long story to tell, but..." She paused in hesitation. Then she changed the course of the topic and demanded, "Can't we be friends again?" She paused waiting for him to reply.

He answered, "Yes, certainly. You were my dear friend, you're my friend and you shall be my friend today, tomorrow and for keeps." It was true. He didn't forget her. Many a time she bobbed up in his mind's eye, only regretting that it was a past story.

Once again the tears that welled up in her eyes said more than words how grateful she felt towards him. They spoke for long.

The sun had gone down some time ago. For a moment, they both stayed wordless and looked at the floor ahead as if none of them had a word to say. Then Anamika looked at her watch pointedly when Animesh exclaimed, "Oh, you're getting late."

"Yes, I am. I've got to go a long way back," she said.

"Sure thing," He said and got up and went into his bedroom, got his mobile and called out a driver.

Hriday turned up in no time. "You have a great job to do, Hriday," he said. "You have to reach Madam back at home in Kanchannagar. I'm giving you what it takes."

Anamika protested, "No, no, you don't have to worry. My taxi is waiting outside."

"Oh, fine then," he said to Anamika and turning to Hriday he said, I'm extremely sorry, Hriday. I didn't know of this. I bothered you for no reason." He apologized. Hriday felt uneasy at his being so polite. "No, no, sir, it's all right. It doesn't matter." He said and went out.

Anamika called the driver to bring the taxi to Animesh's outside door. He saw her off at her taxi. "Take care of yourself," She said in an earnest tone of her soft voice.

"You too, take care and don't worry. See you again if possible." Animesh replied. They both waved at each other as the taxi began to roll slowly. "Call me at your convenience." He said aloud.

He walked slowly back into his room with an inexpressible gladness but thought more seriously, "Why ever did she rush up to here after so many years when I'm in another world!

Chapter 2

The two renewed friends had been in touch with each other since then on the phone. One day she saw him in person again; this time at Jeerat Station. At the farthest platform, No.4, they sat on a concrete bench under the long shade. The place was almost lonely. She spoke about her anguished life in course of conversation. By and by Animesh learnt the 'long story' of hers. The more he listened, the more his heart melted for the innocent woman. While listening to her stories he clucked his tongue time and again. "That's too bad on you," he said sympathetically. "It's quite unbelievable that it happened to you—such a good lady." He took a gentle look at her martyred face for which anyone would feel sorry to see. He added, "Maybe God in heaven has got something good for you. In the Geeta it says: 'Things that happen, happen for the best'. Perhaps, we the small fry can't reach deep enough to understand it."

"I wonder if that's the way it is for me, too," Anamika said half in hope and half in haze.

"I happen to feel it that way, certainly. You'll see it will bring the good for you today or tomorrow."

"How else will anything good happen to me? It doesn't get into my head." Anamika said unbelievably. "I have already passed twelve years this way."

"Maybe, we've got to wait more, and patiently. God's plan we the little people can't know." He said convincingly.

Anamika had the full faith in God and her religion but what pierced her deeply was that the relationship with Bilash reached in such a stage in the long period of time that she lost almost all of her attraction to him. Her heart spontaneously turned harder and harder with the time—just the way the sediment under the deep of the sea turned into limestone from the extreme pressure on it. Many a time she got angry in mind to remember his name.

With the passage of time, the two friends got closer enough. They went and walked about the park on the Hoogly River View Park, and the Bandel Church. They also visited the ISKCON temple at Mayapur because Animesh was specially attracted by ISKCON. Exchanging their thoughts, ideas, and evaluation of life stories, they felt light and comfort in their mind. They both discovered one another afresh. At one time, again, he began to see her face floating in the air ahead of him like what he had seen during the year-long session in college back then.

By and by, it reached her mother's ears. She felt too bad about it and tried to convince her quite a few times about the danger of 'the so-called friendship' because she rightly realized that the friendship of today would turn into more than that from where she couldn't tear herself away. She reminded her of the Hindu custom of marriage. Once married, a dedicated Hindu woman could never think of marrying again and giving herself away to another man even if her husband was separated or in heaven. She also reminded her of the society they belonged to. It'd be defaming for their family. She listened to her mother right but didn't seem to have taken it that much and thus she didn't indicate positive to her mother's suggestions. This indifference about the serious matter made her worry even more. At last, she talked about it to her big daughter, Konika. She worked for India Post.

One day Konika came to see her mainly to talk about the allegation. She spoke for a long time and tried to convince her the same way. Anamika tried to represent Animesh just as a true friend but Konika warned her: "Friendship is alright, but it should be in the place of friendship only if you can be strict enough to get along with this rule. But in all the cases none of the friends can stay in their specified places. That's when the trouble stands out to engulf the peace of both families." She spoke many more things although she couldn't tell her anything emphatically because she too wasn't that much confident about the rejoining of the couple's long-torn relationship. Anamika strongly believed and declared that she was in the limit of the friendship with Animesh.

On the contrary, Animesh's feeling of humanity and morality often warned him off mingling with her any deeper because he leant towards the ISKCON. The still small voice in him occasionally reminded him that he was no longer meant for the married life. It dated him. He was on Lord Krishna's way to be a devotee. He already quit non-veg food. He often shook his head and said to himself, "It's not right, it's not moral to get along with her like this." But the trouble was that he couldn't shrink away from her; some invisible power pulled him towards her, made him think of her. Not a single day could he get by without remembering her face, without thinking of her.

Maybe the same way her feeling affected herself. Her mother and her sister's words rang in her ears and put her down enough. Anyway none of them could just swear it to each other or shrink away. In all truth, this mental fight tore them both from the two ends of their positions. It was a crisis for them both.

For two weeks, both of them overcame the urge to call one another and waited. Animesh asked himself, "Did she think the same way as I do? Or is she ill?" These questions came around several times in his head but he couldn't call her back and ask her. He was in such an uneasy situation. He waited two more weeks—if she'd call him. Nothing happened. At last, it was Animesh who called her over the phone.

Chapter 3

The taxi was in the last quarter to the destination. She was going over to Jeerat from the last call. Only two days before again her mother and her sister's husband tried to convince her about the friendship with Animesh. While thinking about what her mother and sister's husband had told her, she felt drowsy.

The taxi kept running. Suddenly, her mobile trilled rousing her out of the drowsiness. She didn't feel like getting the phone at the moment. So, she let it ring away in her purse on the seat. About a minute later the phone rang again. This time she took it out. It wasn't from any familiar number. She pressed the red button annoyingly and cut it off because she didn't want to be disturbed now.

Immediately the phone rang again stubbornly. She took it out again and noticed that it was the same unknown number. She received it now. Suddenly, she was startled and felt unprepared as the voice from the other side said, "Hello! Who's that? Ana?" It was the most familiar voice she could never fail to recognize; the only person who used to call her by this shortened name of 'Ana'. Yes, it was from Bilash—her husband from so far away after so many years. At first she became nervous and couldn't answer, only held the mobile on her ear—partly confused, partly surprised.

"Hello! Can ye hear me, Ana?" Bilash asked busily with nervousness mixed in his tone.

"Yes, go on," Anamika replied plainly. "First of all, give me your word that you'll listen to me intently, please!" He urged sincerely and paused for her answer. He didn't ask about her—how she was, how her parents were—how was everything—although he called her after the many years. It was because of his guilty-consciousness. He knew how he left her out then when he was deeply under the hypnotism of the white-skinned Swedish woman and the temptation for a Swedish citizenship.

Now it was time for Anamika to take on her vanity. "Why? What do you want after so many years?" She asked gravely.

"Please, please! I'll tell you everything," he said quickly. "That's why I called you up, dear! Please, give me the time it needs," he said appealingly and made a short pause.

"Dear am I! To you!" She said ironically with a touch of surprise. "How ridiculous!"

Bilash got a little puzzled at this. He tried to make it up. "Please, please," he said repeatedly. "Please, listen to me with a bit of patience. Please!"

She had a mixed feeling of confusion and pleasing excitement to have a call from her so-long-beloved husband who didn't even receive her call at one time, who didn't remember her all along the years she had been left like that. She felt a slight shiver running through her body. After some time, she felt uneasy because she couldn't hear the voice clearly from the noise of the car. She held her phone away and asked the driver to stop by the side.

"Are you there, Ana?" He asked again. "I am. Go ahead," she said being tempted to hear him out. Bilash kept on speaking.

The long-isolated couple had a long talk on the mobile on the move at first, then at a halt, parking the car by the road in the open field with the rows of young trees on both sides and sending the driver over to the nearby tea kiosk. It was close to a crossroads.

Mostly Bilash was the speaker and Anamika the listener. His call of an explanatory talk after so long time melted the ice to some extent, right, but she was more concerned now. She felt herself like the rope of the tug of war.

Her journey had to be put off for the day with some acceptable excuse to Animesh. She decided to turn back home.

All the way back she was deeply thoughtful. What a lot of things, what a lot of ways she thought. She wondered if she could trust her again, if he was just conning her and would slide away again with some new opportunities like what he did for the many years for which she had to suffer so much and spoiled her life. This crucial question came round big to her. And it was only him that was responsible for the whole of the miseries. Now she learnt that he obtained his cherished citizenship of Sweden, which meant he wouldn't step into India other than a short visit. She couldn't calm down in mind. She was in bewilderment.

While thinking and thinking, he went back home from there, the night came down, it grew young, then younger. She hit the sack. But, both deep concern and excitement brought her a night of broken sleep. Most of the night she spent awake or sleep came to her in brief snatches. She could hear the tick-tock of the big wall clock in the pin-drop silence in the dimly-lit room, sometimes street dogs barking outside on the road or far away in the still winter night. She recalled Bilash's melting words; asking to be pardoned, to be accepted back and be loved back and cared. He promised to be tied to her for the rest of the years of his life. She kept on thinking with the night toward its end.

Anyway the night wore away this way. The dawn chorus was caught in her ears. She let the sun rise up; she lay half-asleep, and half awake in bed, exhausted. In the back of her mind she prayed, "Lord Krishna, please, show me the proper way; what I should do. Be kind on me, please!"

Chapter 4

A week later Anamika met Animesh at River Park. When Animesh heard about Bilash's unexpected call to her across from the continent after so many years, he felt a jolt to his heart. He was afraid to think that there was a good possibility for the isolated couple to be re-united and she may get away from him for ever. His face suddenly shrunk and turned blue which didn't escape her notice.

It certainly was despondent to him no matter how differently he thought of her or made up his mind because in reality, things were different—they both came closer and closer. It couldn't be in its limit. But he didn't let out what it felt him like beneath him. Or rather, he expressed a mode of happiness. He encouraged her. "Oh, wonderful, Anamika! It's a piece of very good news," he said with a big artificial enthusiastic smile at her. Anamika was in confusion. So, she just let out a small dry smile in answer and thought to herself, "Who knows how good it is."

"It will be good, I think. I told you, 'things will change'—they did; they have to, because of the turning of the time-wheel of the universe," he said wisely. "The same season can't stay all year long in a region. Our life is like so."

Although it felt her good to have a few more calls from Bilash in the meantime, but still somewhere in the core of her heart, she still felt sort of scared. She'd lost her faith on that man. More to the point, how could she quit her job and leave her country leaving her parents alone in the house? She was in two minds about taking a decision.

Animesh tried to inspire her to get ahead up the way to Bilash's will. Because he had to. He convinced her in many ways to forget the past and accept the present. He said, "Look, Anamika, one of the most important things that you ought to realize is that a woman needs a man to support her and stand up very like a wall at the frontier of a country. Just as a man without a woman is not perfect, the same way, a woman without a man is never complete. A woman needs a man to care for her, and a man needs a woman to look after him. It's the reciprocal needs and desires." Here Anamika thought of Animesh being imperfect as well without a woman in his life but it would only point back at her. So, she kept silent and let Animesh continue.

"If you want to get your husband back of your own, then, not just from here can you bring him back—you'll have to go over to him right there up to—what-d'you-call-it?" Animesh stumbled into a short pause, "Er..., Stockholm—yeah, Stockholm and live with him to reach yourself close to his heart and let him come close to yours. It's never possible being left out so far away from each other. Then you can bring him back sooner or later." Anamika listened to him like a good girl. Animesh went on.

"Just as a desert—if it receives rain over and over again, it becomes juicy and turn into fertile soil, so does the heart—if it gets enough love from somebody, it turns to be a loving one. And if it doesn't receive love and care, it becomes as hard and dry as a rocky plateau." He didn't mention his heart was an example to it.

Here Anamika opened her mouth: "That's the way I got along with him since I got married, but..." She couldn't speak; her voice broke from strong saddened emotion, her head leaned down covering her face in her hands. Tears welled up in her eyes and brimmed over. He let her weep for a moment. "That's how misunderstanding happens to be a disaster by and by," Animesh said sympathetically sharing a part of her distress. "Be cool! Be cool!" he paused and again said, "Calm down, Anamika. Calm down, be cool."

Soon she managed the surge of emotion, and wiping the tears she continued, "He didn't want to relate me. I'd tried my hardest to hold him back but he was determined about his decision and slipped out of my grip.

"I didn't know why I'd had an ominous signal in the heart that'd made me sort of restive and fearful then. The more I tried to convince him, the more he became aggressive to me. Even when I'd called to him out there, he was more aggressive and wouldn't receive my call. And then he went beyond my reach. It was that woman, yes that Freja Nielson ate him up." She wiped her eyes again with her sari end.

"Anyway, what's gone gone. Now, listen to me good." He leaned a little forward. "As a true friend, as you have taken me for, I'll never misguide you." He paused shortly and then said, "When he's changed his mind and turned towards you, he must have had enough of unpleasant experiences on the foreign land. And it's almost certain that he won't do the same blunder again. So far I know about the Western world's women—some of them are not trustable for a conjugal family life. They just would come to one's life either to squeeze out money as much as possible or just to play around with the man for physical pleasure. Maybe he fell into the grip of one of the 'some', unfortunately." He paused shortly.

"Now the time has come. God has smiled on you again after you've gone through the hardest tests on miseries. You're not supposed to push your luck. Take it from me. Fly over to him. I'll do what it takes to help you out with this matter." She looked up at his face again when Animesh said, "Yes, it had been my promise I'd always be to help you; not to harm."

Chapter 5

The thing was that she would no way want to quit her job and leave her parents, and also because she was scared to be alone helplessly out there. At the same time she felt too weak to travel across the continent—she was a woman after all. Anyway, it took him a lot of effort to get her to agree to go over to Bilash to Sweden.

At last, she agreed when Bilash reassured her that he would no way let her be in trouble on the way. He kept his word. He helped her all the way to get to the mission—getting her the passport and visa done, shopping the necessary things she needed on the way and out there, and so on.

Twelfth of April, Anamika was out on lien leave on the eeriest journey of her maiden tour on the airplane. Naturally, there was a sad ambience in the taxi as it was running down the Express Way to Calcutta airport. Anamika was going to re-mingle with her husband. So, she was to have been more pleased than ever but the vicious tension masked up her pleasure—the only thing bobbed up in her head—she was going so far away all by herself. Also she was worried about her parents although her elder sister took care of them.

Animesh felt the sweet smell of mango blossom in his nose wafted by the breeze as it was passing by big mango orchards on either side. He sniffed eagerly and exclaimed, "Wow! Wonderful smell, from the mango orchard." Anamika too got the smell but she wasn't in the mood of feeling it enjoyably from the concern. She only slightly nodded her head in agreement with Animesh. "This means your journey would be happy and nice," he said looking up at her.

"Why?" Anamika asked softly. "Sweet smell always indicates the goodness," he replied.

"I wish it would be so," she said and went silent. The journey took about three hours.

She felt a sudden shaft of cold under her chest as she got into the airport through the big gate up to the parking lot; the big sign of Netaji Airport Calcutta caught in her eyes.

After she'd gone through the luggage-weight and booking and immigration check-ins step by step at different counters, she had been waiting with Animesh at the waiting lounge hearing the announcement of the arrivals and departures of aeroplanes to and from different international and domestic cities. They stayed wordless more often than they spoke.

The two faces of the two friends looked gloomy like the monsoon sky with grey clouds. One face showed worries evidently painted on it wondering 'who knows what the hell's gonna happen' and the other one showed an impression of sadness from losing the found-back friend—but he tried fruitlessly not to let it stand out on his face.

"You still seem to be worrying, why?" Animesh asked, his eyes went searchingly at her face. "Everything has been arranged properly." Animesh guessed all his reassurance, injecting guts into her didn't work that much. It was quite natural though. Animesh himself couldn't have escaped this aggression either.

"It does happen, Animesh-da," she replied softly. "You wouldn't know how hard it is for a woman to deal with a situation single-handed, especially out of home so far away."

"Don't take it that way. Think of them—European women who are travelling alone across the world," Animesh said emphatically.

"They're smarter than us. They are used to travelling alone right from their adolescence, besides they know English very well that you need most," Anamika replied.

"But your case is different. Your husband will be there to receive you at the airport. I know how eagerly he is waiting to receive you. I know it from the sound he talked to me. He will do all to welcome you.

All you have to do is get your documents ready at hand and produce them as the airport officials ask for."

If he doesn't turn up in the end ...?" She asked with a touch of fun through her worries and tried to let out a mischievous smile looking into his eyes. It was perhaps the last ever fun he had from Anamika.

"That's it," he said right away. "In that case, call me over, you wicked! I'll fly out over to you and rescue you and take you back home." He made a funny laugh. She too joined the laugh saying, "Will you? Honest!?"

"Actions speak louder than words, my dear," he answered. In the back of his mind he said, "If that was possible, who the hell would let you out on the way to cross the continent!"

"I know, Mr. Bhabook," she said with a wry smile. All the same, at one time she thought she had better not go. Rather, if she had a way, she'd have cried off and gone back home and lived all by herself, but there was no way now. Her head felt heavy and painful. What a lot of things bobbed up in her mind now—if the plane crashed, or captured by hijackers or be left out from technical problems on the mid-way at Dubai or Vienna, and so on!

After they had eaten at the restaurant, they had been waiting for the boarding announcement. The more the time came nearer, the eerier she felt. Animesh could realize how she felt at that moment. He happened to remember the same feeling of the time when he'd stepped out for Bombay all alone. He could picture the eerie situations at mid-night at Mankhurd station and the short journey from there to the Dutt Mandir after midnight in an Auto-rickshaw through the jungle and the bad experiences from the local loafers that had happened to him factually.

He now closed his eyes for a moment and opened again to look at her face. "I know how you feel, friend," he said sympathetically. "Be strong and confident in your mind. You'll win. Remember, gaining something through hard labour and difficulties is sweeter than gaining something easily." He tried to instill guts into her.

"I know," she pronounced plainly but not weakly. "Once I have jumped into the waters, I'll sink or swim," she said resignedly.

"You'll swim, I bet. You'll be able to swim over to the island, no matter how far it is. God will be with you to guide you to your destination. Because it's destined by God himself."

Between their talks, the announcement came for the passengers to board the plane. It was 16:15 then. "There it is!" Animesh said. "You gotta be going." They both stood up from their seats slowly, as if, Anamika not feeling enthusiastic and Animesh not wanting to let her off; but still he'd have to let her go was the inevitability. "So, it is time..." She said softly.

"Yes, it is..." he replied. She was about to move to the plane when there was an exchange of looks between the two friends which was filled with an inexpressible feeling for each other." Take care of yourself, Animesh-da," she said staring at his face pitifully.

"I will, Anamika," answered Animesh. "And you too." He handed her a gift-packed pen. He had a strong feeling that he mightn't see her in this life again. She mightn't like to come back from there either.

She thanked him, slowly walked to the staircase. She looked back, and waved to him and he to her, and then she walked up the stairs with her soaked eyes letting him stare at her back, the gift-pack held in her hand.

Sitting in the seat, she opened the gift-pack and found a nice pen in it and a small slip with the message: "I only wish I would get you of my own in the next life and devote ourselves to the feet of Lord Krishna. I'll be waiting."

"I will, too," she breathed out looking down at the message. Tears welled up in her eyes once again blurring the handwritten message.

_____ **The end**

Disclaimer

The Destined Destinies is fabricated romantic story. It has not been intended for any particular person or persons. If any of the characters of this book does match with any person or persons, it may have happened only by coincidence. The writer of the book does not deserve to be accused.

Sushen K. Biswas

Acknowledgement

I am very much grateful to Draft2Digital for letting me a grand opportunity to publish my books (two in number) and let them go across the world for readers to avail them.

Sushen K. Biswas

Don't miss out!

Visit the website below and you can sign up to receive emails whenever Sushen Biswas publishes a new book. There's no charge and no obligation.

https://books2read.com/r/B-A-DBXNC-FZNCF

BOOKS 2 READ

Connecting independent readers to independent writers.

About the Author

About the author

The author of the book .Sushen Biswas 'The Destined Destinies' was born in 1966 in West Bengal, India in a poor family and got thorugh hard times for education. He became a teacher at a school in West Bengal 11 years late. During his unemployment he did private tutions and learned English specifically, at unit institute of Oxford English World Service in Katwa and by and by he was tempted to write something in English. This book is one of his two published books.